THE TRUTH CAN'T BE HIDDEN

THE SECRET OF AKHEL CAVES

GOPI MANOJ

The Truth Can't Be Hidden
Fiction by Gopi Manoj

First Impression: October 2019

© Gopi Manoj

ISBN: 978-9389244274

Published by: Writersgram Publications, New Delhi

www.writersgram.com
publications@writersgram.com

Gopi Manoj asserts the moral right to be identified as the author of this book.

ACKNOWLEDGEMENT

The book that you are holding in your hands is my dream. Whenever I see the famous quote *"If you can dream it you can do it"* by Walt Disney, I get confidence that I can achieve my dream one day. There are some people in this world; some of them are wonderful that made this dream become a product that you are holding in your hand. I would like to thank them all and there are a few names that I have to mention them:

Datta Sai – He is the ink of my pen. He used to support me and encourage me whenever I fail and gave good ideas and suggestions. I am very proud to have such a good and supportive friend in my life.

Sri Lekha, Fariyal, Meghana, Mounika, Dimple, and Eswar – great friends who read the manuscript and gave me some honest comments. They also helped me in boosting my confidence while writing this book with their suggestions.

And lastly my publisher, Deepanshu Gupta sir, the MD of Writersgram publications who helped me in achieving my dream. He is friendly and encouraged me throughout my process of achieving my dream.

ABOUT THE AUTHOR

Gopi Manoj is a 22-year old Indian author who debuted with his book "The Truth Can't Be Hidden: The Secret of Akhel Caves". He is a software engineer working in TCS at Banglore. He aims to write in simple English which can be understood by all ages of people. He likes writing adventures and science fiction novels. He is very active on social media and you can connect him on his Instagram.

Connect with Gopi Manoj via his:

Instagram profile: @authorgopimanoj

Website: www.authorgopimanoj.in

PROLOGUE

Can India lift the U-19 world cup again? Can Datta be the hero for India? What if Aussies will again dominate the show? Only an over left to answer all the questions. Here comes Ben, he has already defended 5 off the last over in the semis, can he do it again?

Datta on strike, India need 14 off 6.

Ben [9.0-3-35-2] is back into the attack.

The Aussie captain is adjusting the field. Fielders outside the 30-yard circle on the off-side are called off. Four fielders are placed inside the 30-yard circle of off-side.

49.1 Ben to Datta, Datta! Banged through the covers. But, the fielder in the cover region dived towards his left and slowed down the pace of the ball and the ball rolled towards the deep cover. Datta could only get a couple of the first ball.

49.2 Ben to Datta, 1 run, a bouncer and Datta pulled the ball but he finds a fielder at the deep square leg.

11 from 4 required. Kumar on the strike, he can be a hero today for India. Long-off has been called off and a fielder is placed in the deep cover.

49.3 Ben to Kumar, 1run, hammered it straight to extra cover. Only a single is added to the tally.

49.4 Ben to Datta, a wide Yorker. Ben and the wicket - keeper made a quick appeal but the umpire did not raise his finger. Datta had hit the ground but not the ball.

India is in serious trouble now, India needs 10 of 2. Again, it's going to be a nail-biter tonight.

49.5 Ben to Datta, what is going to happen on this delivery? It's wide Yorker again, but Datta made no mistake now and banged over deep extra cover. 6 runs added to the scoreboard.

The last ball of the world cup, India need 4 of the final delivery. All the hopes are on Datta, can India defeat the Aussies. A boundary of the last ball, India wins the world cup. If 3 runs are scored we are going to have a super-over in this super final.

49.6 Ben to Datta, Datta! Dataaaaaaaaaa! It is a bouncer Datta pulled the ball across the deep square leg, it is a six, celebrations began and India wins the world cup.

Datta is called up and the presenter took a small interview for his lightning performance tonight. There is a huge celebration going on in the stadium and mostly in India. The boys were called for the trophy presentation. Datta is given the man of the match and the player of the series award for his all-round performance. The captain is given the cup and the boys joined him and lifted the cup.

❖❖❖❖❖

Hello all, I am Varun and welcome back to your favorite show *'It's My Story"* with a new season. Before we start, a very happy national sports day to all the viewers. So let us start the new season with an all-rounder in his life. He is a topper of IIT, space traveller, CID informer and the winner of U-19 cricket world cup. He achieved all this at an age of 18 and he is none other than India's all-rounder Datta. So, Let's welcome Datta to our show!

Varun: Welcome Datta welcome to the show "It's My Story".

Datta: Thank you, sir, for inviting me for the show and I am proud to be here as a guest in the show.

Varun: First of congratulations on winning the U-19 world cup and Man of the tournament award.

Datta: Thank you, sir.

Varun: Tell me how do you feel about winning the world cup.

Datta: Firstly, I feel very happy about getting the chance in the team. Secondly, I used to dream every day about winning the world cup for our country. Finally, I have achieved my dream with the support of my friends and Sachin sir. I feel very happy for achieving such a great feat in my teenage.

Varun: What was your plan, how did you play the last over?

Datta: My plan was very simple sir. Concentrating on one ball at a time and during the last over I didn't look at the scoreboard and I concentrated on each and every ball. But I felt much tensed on the last ball. So, once I looked at my friends before playing the ball and then I scored the winning six.

Varun: You are a topper; cricketer and you do a lot of adventures. Don't you feel difficulty in managing all these?

Datta: Handling all these is very difficult sir but by friends, especially Heidi, help me a lot in handling all these things.

Varun: Ok Datta tell me about your journey from getting admitted into IIT to winning the world cup.

Datta: It's a long journey of one year sir. There are many setbacks, challenges, moments of joy and moments of misery but I overcame all these with my friends. It all started on my first day to IIT.

FIRST DAY AT IIT

College is a dreamland for all those who got tired with disciplined and restricted life of their school. Once college begins, they feel like they have won the war and got independence, and like many students, I thought the same. It is a beautiful period and shows a picture of learning, enjoyment, freedom, and friendship. They weave an everlasting impact on human memory. Each moment we spend in a college is worth-living, enjoyable and worth-remembering. The first day at college is really very special and memorable for every student. In fact, the joys and freedom that were a dream in the School become a reality in college.

It was half past six. Half of the city was awake. Housewives were out with their kids armed with Tiffin box and water bottles waiting for the school bus. I could hear some prayer chants of Lord Shiva from the temple. My eyes were open as I was awake from the restful slumber and memories of the past day were new to me for a few moments before the events rush back to my mind. I then realized where I was and what day it was. While my brain wakes up and I become aware of everything, I burrow down deeper under the thick, inviting sheets and sink into the memory foam pad as the sun peeks through the blinds. Fuzzy blankets coil around my legs and wish me to stay, to not leave its comforting embrace. Yet, as resisting as it is, I let my naked feet fall to the chilled wooden floor, and the morning breeze from the open window touched my legs.

I didn't waste a single minute, got down from the bed, and finished brushing and bathing quickly. I put on the blue shirt, as I prefer it as lucky. Meanwhile, my mother cooked a delicious breakfast. I took a pair of new notebooks and stationery, put them in my bag, and went to the dining room. I ate some riots and drank some milk. Looking at my nervous face, my father came to me and said *don't panic, all the things pass on, just be calm and enjoy the life.* After listening to his words, I felt very happy and relaxed. I took blessings from them and started going to college, which was half a mile away from my house.

In the middle, I stopped at my school's main gate and recollected all the memories. I can still remember the first day when I was crying at the gate while my mother was leaving me, the punishments that I got when I was improper to the school. But, most importantly, I could remember my social science teacher, she was inspirational to me. She used to be friendly and used to take special care of me.

As I was about to leave, a car came towards the main gate and stopped near me. I was eagerly looking to see who it might be and to my surprise, she was my social science teacher. She called me and asked me to get in the car. Soon we went to the staff room, I could see all the teachers and some new faces there. I went to everyone and all appreciated me for getting admission in IIT and especially my social science teacher. I took blessings from them and then I looked around the school and left for IIT.

❖❖❖❖❖

It was half-past 8 when I reached the IIT main gate. Many students dream and work hard to get admission in an IIT and I was one among them. I remember the promise I made to my sister Sri Lekha 2 years ago to get admission into an IIT. She is currently working as a CID officer in crime department. The moment I stepped into the college was the most remarkable in my life. I felt like I achieved something great in my life. My emotions were like a new place and a new life with a new lifestyle.

There was a great hustle and bustle in the college. I found myself among many students who were looking happy but I could see some fear hiding in their eyes like me. Everyone feared about ragging because in recent years, many students committed suicide due to harassment by seniors. The main objective of ragging is to *'break the ice'* between seniors and new entrants. But over generations, it is done disorderly by torturing students both mentally and physically.

The seniors were sitting over the benches at the entrance and were eagerly waiting for the juniors. I was made to stand in a queue and 1 could see two boys and two girls who were taking an introduction from students. The boy in front of me was asked to sing first, and then they asked him to take off his shirt and make 50 rounds around them. He started crying and they laughed and told him to leave.

Now it was my turn, I felt nervous and one of them called me.

"Hey, giraffe come over here and tell me about yourself".

I paused for a moment and started "I am Datta, an under-19 Mumbai cricketer hailing from Powai. I completed my schooling from St. Peters school" and I was about to continue when a boy among them asked me to stop and said *"Hello Datta don't you remember me, I am Kishore your friend from childhood."*

After listening to that name, I felt very happy because Kishore was my senior in the school and he was the person behind my passion for cricket. Kishore taught me how to play the game of cricket and we used to play gully cricket during my schooling. He took me to the canteen and ordered a soft drink to relieve my tension.

"Don't worry Datta, even I faced the same situation during my first year. I am currently 3rd year student here and pursuing computers and captain of the college cricket team and Mumbai Ranji player." I still was in surprise because after 5 years, I met him and we talked some time and exchanged numbers.

"If you face any problem, call me and mess with anyone but don't mess with our seniors and I am having my practice session and I will meet you in the evening."

It was 9' O clock and I heard an announcement saying *"all the newcomers are requested to join the welcome party at the seminar hall of humanities block within 10 minutes."*

One of the most impressive traditions that IIT's follow was throwing a welcome party for the new students. It was an emotional gathering, the moment I entered the seminar hall I could see a huge gathering of students. The hall was big enough to accommodate 1000 members; it was surrounded with large speakers and centralized air conditioning. Our seniors being the hosts, started with the prayer song, then some of them came forward and shared their experiences. But most of the boys were eying the female anchor for her looks and her melodious voice.

The principal took over and addressed us with some helpful instructions and cracked some jokes to relieve the fear in us. The most important thing I can remember is giving some appreciation prizes for the top rankers, and luckily I was one among them. While I was about to leave the stage, the principal stopped me and asked me to say a few words. I have a little bit of stage fear and I was thinking of what to say, then I remembered the story that my sister told me. So, I began!

'Once in a village, there lived two brothers Ramu and Somu who inherited their father's 2 acres of land. It was divided among them equally and both started harvesting wheat. After a few years, Ramu got married, had children and Somu was still enjoying a bachelor's life. One night Somu thought to himself, *"It is not fair to have equal land. Since my childhood, he is looking after me and he has 2 children to feed and I was alone. So he should have more grain to look after them"*.

So that night, Somu went to his silo and took a large bag of wheat with him and went over to his brother's farm silo, leaving wheat in his brother's silo. Somu returned home happily by paying the debt for his brother for all his love.

Same night Ramu was also lying awake thinking, *"It is not fair to have equal land. In my old age, my wife and I will have our grown children to take care of us while my brother has none. So he must have more grains to sell so he can live happily in old age."*

He also secretly went to his silo and then climbed to his brother's silo and left bags of wheat there. He returned happily after helping his brother.

Next morning both of them were surprised and confused by seeing the same number of wheat bags in their own silo. So both of them thought that, *"Tonight, I will be sure to take more wheat to brother's farm."*

After the night fell, each brother gathered a great amount of wheat from his barn and in the dark, secretly delivered it to his brother's barn.

Next morning both of them were puzzled to see the number of wheat bags remained constant. So both of them thought that, *"That's impossible! Tonight, I will make no mistake and make sure that grains are delivered."*

The third night, each brother gathered a large pile of wheat from his silo and loaded it on to a cart and slowly moved it to brother's barn. In the mid-way under the shadow of the moon, each brother recognized the other and realized what happened. Without saying a word, they both walked away and started living together and happily.

The moral is *"We should love and respect our family. The happiness of giving is much greater than taking."*

So, my dear friends where ever you go and where ever you live respect your family because without their support you would not have been at this stage.

After listening to the story, all the people stood and applauded me, especially our principal and head of the department. Then we were divided into our respective streams and assigned a teacher to show us around the college. An old lady named Sana was assigned to us. She first took us to our computer department and showed us all the labs, classrooms then to various blocks, the library and finally she took us to the playground. IIT has a huge playground with two cricket grounds, football stadiums, basketball courts, tennis courts, indoor stadium and especially the swimming pool to practice. I felt very happy by seeing all this as I did not see such a big playground in my early life.

Later we were sent to our respective classes, I could see myself surrounded by 59 other familiar faces. We all were busy in talking to our peers until a bald headed man entered the class. He was our department head and told about the college and then gave some rules and left the class. Soon, our classes began and most of the classes went about introducing ourselves and some teachers shared their experiences with our seniors. Once a teacher asked me to introduce myself and I started as usual but the moment when I said I was a U-19 cricketer, the entire class was shocked.

❖❖❖❖❖

It was a 4'o clock in the evening, all my classes were over and I was about to leave the college when suddenly I got a call from Kishore bro and he told me to meet him in the canteen. I immediately went to canteen there he was waiting for me and asked me to follow him. I didn't understand where he was taking me and quietly followed. After walking certain yards we reached college ground. He said me take the ball and bowl for him. I bowled a few overs to him and later he bowled to me. Later he said *"Soon you will be having selections for the college team for an inter-college cricket tournament and I wish you to participate in it and I will intimate you about it in advance and prepare well for the selections."*

I felt very happy and later we moved to college mess and there we had some snacks and sat on the benches outside the hostel. I was thinking to ask him about the female anchor I saw today but held my nerves because it might be odd. Seeing me, he asked *"do you want to ask me anything Datta?"* *"Actually, I want to ask you about the female anchor of the morning's function"* I said. He laughed and told me that she was Filomina and she has a huge following in college but she ignores all so don't mess with her, he warned me.

While we were talking I saw a girl who was sitting next to our bench and I showed her to Kishore and he insisted me to tease her. I felt very nervous because I don't even know how to speak properly to girls. But he forced me and I called her from distance. She was tall, nearly equal to my height and thin. She had kohl-black curly hair, saccharine sweet lips, attractive eyes with white skin tone and looking so simple. She looked traditional with her dressing and appearance. She came towards me and asked, *"tell me brother what do you want"*. I was impressed by her sweet voice and asked her to sing.

She felt very nervous and started singing and then I asked her to tell her about herself. She told me that her name was Jahnavi and she was from Andhra Pradesh and her father was working in ISRO. But I didn't know what to ask and told her to leave and she left. Kishore bro saw me and understood I have fallen for her. After a few minutes, I got a call from my mother and I saw it was a 6'o clock and I left for home.

At the end of the first day, I returned home. When I was returning home, all the memories of my first day at College came to my mind. It was like a movie. It had fun and fear. I remembered all the happenings and reached home with a smile. I told everything that happened to my mother and she laughed at me by listening that I teased a girl. I ate my dinner and went to sleep.

❖❖❖❖❖

FINDING NEW RELATIONS

India is in serious trouble, 8 wickets down and it needs to score 19 off final over to win the U-19 world cup. All hopes are on Datta; will he take India on the winning side or will it be West Indies' show again.

Thakur is on strike and India needs 19 off 6.

Thomas [9.0-2-15-3] is back into the bowling attack.

49.1 Thomas to Thakur, bowled! Thomas cleans him up. It's in block hole, Thakur couldn't defend it and loses his middle stump. There's check on no-ball but everything is fine.

Thakur b Thomas 10(15)

Manoj, the right-handed batsman, comes to the crease

49.2 Thomas to Manoj, 1 run, full at the stumps, missed his length but Manoj misuses and plays down the ground between long-on and long-off. Datta rejects for the second one to keep his strike.

49.3 Thomas to Datta, SIX, OH MY GOD! This is gigantic. It's gone out of the park. A full toss and Datta uses it and he clears the boundary over long-on. We can see the fire in his eyes. It's 110-meter six. Indian fans got some hope and started cheering.

49.4 Thomas to Datta, one more SIX, this time over long-off to brings his CENTURY off just 80 balls but he didn't celebrate. Tries a

Yorker but misses it at least by a couple of feet and Datta lofts it with enough power - if not timing - to clear long-off.

Windies were in serious trouble now, India needs 6 of 2. Captain and wicket-keeper went to Thomas and discussing. Indian fans started cheering Datta! Datta!

49.5 Thomas to Datta, what's going to be this delivery? It's a Yorker, no run, doesn't take the single this time either. Datta looks to muscle it with a flat-batted smite but doesn't get any timing. Limply struck to long-on.

The last ball of the world cup, India need six of the final delivery. All hopes on Datta, can India defeat the defending champions.

49.6 Thomas to Datta, It's a bouncer, Datta pushes it to the third man, there is a fielder underneath it but, can't hold it and the ball has crossed the ropes. But on-field umpire is not sure whether the ball has crossed without stepping and sends it for 3rd umpire's decision. The third umpire checked the ball from various camera views and was ready with his decision. The entire world was looking for this decision, Datta looked confident and the empire was about to give decision suddenly alarm rings Tik! Tik! Tik! Shit, this alarm always disturbs my dreams.

It has been two weeks since I joined IIT but still, I didn't find a friend. Every day waking up, eating then going to IIT, attending classes then playing sometime in the ground and returning home and again eating and sleeping. This has been my daily routine which looks like I am again studying class 12. I thought to add some new colours to my life and change this daily routine. So, I began talking to all especially never waste a chance to talk especially to girls.

It was a fine Monday morning just a day after India's independence, a new girl entered into my life. It was a computer programming class, I was busy playing PUBG with my classmates from the beginning of class. Suddenly a girl entered the class and asked

"Excuse me, madam, may I get in?" with her sweet voice.

"Why you are late to the class?" Madam asked

"Madam I have just got shifted from electronics to computers in spot counselling".

All the boys are looking at her but I ignored her and kept playing PUBG in my mobile, it was top 5 and only I was left in my squad.

Madam asked her to introduce herself to the class.

"Hello friends my name is Jahnavi, I am from Andhra Pradesh" she said.

Listening to that, I was shocked and kept my phone down and saw her. I laughed realizing that it was the same girl whom I teased on my first day and concentrated on my game and got chicken dinner, it was my chicken dinner after 100 games and first of the season. I didn't even kill a person but how it is possible, is it her presence that bought me the luck, I questioned myself. I again played a game this time to the same result, I kept on winning the game. My classmates started praising me and requested me to play more games with them. For the first time in my life, I started thinking about the presence of luck in the form of her but ignored it.

Then in the evening, after going home I again started playing the game. One game after other my survival time came decreasing and at one point of time, I was getting killed before landing on the ground. I again asked the same question but this time to ignored thinking it might be an instance.

Two days had passed and I was still struggling to talk to girls, as said: *"every dog has its day"* and my day had come. It was chemistry lab, Sana madam's class and she told us to do titration experiment which has 2 basic levels and 2 advanced levels. So, she decided to group us into pairs so that the experiment will be completed in a less time. She also told us that she will be going to award 20 marks for the pair who completes the experiments successfully within 90 minutes of time.

All the students who were greedy for marks picked students with good marks in the previous lab sessions. Since I had very few scores in my previous sessions, no one came forward to pick me as their partner. Jahnavi was new to class and thus she was also left unpicked. So we both were placed into a team and we occupied the corner of the lab.

Since Jahnavi was new to the lab, she didn't know much about it so I just gave her my notes and asked her to follow it up. But she ignored me due to the incident on the first day and as she was still angry over me. So, I started doing the experiment individually setting up the setup as given in the notes. It took me over 15 minutes to properly set it up. While others had already done setting and started doing titration. I then started adding components one by one. While adding components instead of adding base I added acid and began titrating it. After a few minutes, the conical flask burst into pieces but luckily there was no fire. All the class looked just like we committed a crime and Sana madam told everyone to look into their own business.

She came to me and identified that I added acid instead of a base. She smiled and said *"don't worry Datta mistakes happen while learning."* I felt relieved and started doing the experiment again from the beginning and observed that Jahnavi had just started titrating. I thought to myself that this lab is also gone and I was again going to get the lowest score of the class. Half of the time finished and all the batches completed at least one but we didn't complete one at least. Sana madam identified that we don't have proper communication and were doing experiment individually.

"Dattu and Jahnavi come to me once" she loudly called us.

I thought that we were dead and she will kick us out of the lab and fail me in the lab.

"What's wrong with you guys, why didn't you complete at least one titration?"

I didn't understand what to say and was thinking how to escape from her but suddenly *"Madam I don't want to work with him and I don't like his attitude"* Jahnavi replied without thinking for a moment. By listening that, I was out of words, Sana madam understood the problem.

"Ok, guys I have understood your problem so let me share a small experience of my life. If you still don't want to listen to me it's up to you." She Said.

A 24-year-old boy was watching out from the train's window and shouted…

"Dad, look the trees are going behind!"

Dad smiled and a young couple sitting nearby, looked at the 24-year old's childish behaviour with pity, suddenly he again exclaimed…

"Dad, look the clouds are running with us!"

The couple couldn't resist and said to the old man…

"Why don't you take your son to a good doctor?"

The old man smiled and said… *"I did and we are just coming from the hospital, my son was blind from birth, he just got his eyes today. Every single person on the planet has a story. Don't judge people before you truly know them. The truth might surprise you. We don't know in what situation they are and everything that appears will not be true."*

"So, Datta and Jahnavi, the reason behind this activity is to improve coordination between you and develop teamwork. So if you don't work together now, how will you work in the future" Sana madam said.

We both understood and apologized her and started doing the experiment together. Initially, we failed a couple of times but later we completed one experiment after another. At the end of the lab, we were the only batch to complete both basic level and advanced level experiments and as promised madam gave us 20 marks for successful completion. While leaving, she once again called both of us and asked to redo the experiments of previous sessions after college and prepare a report.

In the evening, after college as madam told, we attended the lab. Since I had an idea of lab, I initially explained things to her and later asked her to do the experiment and I kept writing the lab report. Soon within 90 minutes we managed to complete all the experiments and submitted the report to madam. While going, I thought to say sorry for teasing her and explain the story behind teasing her.

"Jahnavi I am sorry for teasing you on that day."

"No problem Datta and thanks for teaching me how to do experiments" she replied. Then I explained the situation that led me to tease her and she forgave me for misunderstanding me and left for home.

In the evening, every day after going home, I used to open Facebook and talk to my friends, especially my sister. During my college days, I wasn't much of a social butterfly. I roughly had 50-60 friends and most of them were my relatives and family friends. Similarly, after going home I opened Facebook and got a message from my sister and started talking to her. Meanwhile, I got a message from an account named Jahnavi Janu. I got a bit tensed because while I was new to this platform, my sister once sent me a link. When I opened that link my entire system got crashed and I couldn't control my laptop and I was clueless on what was going on and kept my system aside. Then my sister called me and said that she has hacked my system. So I asked her whether she again started playing with me she said she was busy doing some urgent work. So I opened with little fear and saw the message:

"Hello Datta I'm Jahnavi of your class, I need some help."

I relaxed when I realized it was her and replied her back:

"Hello Jahnavi, tell me what can I do for you?"

"Datta, actually I have many doubts regarding subjects. Can you help me out because I'm new to the class and don't know anyone except you."

I understood her situation and agreed to help her after college.

We started talking; slowly at first, then we became closer as I loved talking to her. Every day we both used to go to the college library and I used to explain the concepts I knew. I was terribly honest and straightforward at the time as I did not really talk to people too often and did not really know what I was doing. But, this girl had something special in her that attracted me towards her.

Every day we would message each other, one day she asked me to teach her PUBG. I taught her the game and soon we started playing the game. Initially, she used to make fun while playing the game and soon we became one of the best duos. We had a squad named Dynamos and used to play the game often when we found the time and sometimes even in classes. We had met just a week ago yet we understood each other very clearly.

Slowly we started skipping classes, mostly the English classes and spent time in either canteen or the library. Though we didn't have classes during weekends, I used to go to IIT and we both sat together and talked about some stuff. Sometimes I used to take her to the ground while I was practicing, because she loved cricket and most likely she was a die-hard fan of Rohit Sharma.

As days passed, watching us, some of our classmates started spreading rumours. Some of them used to call us lovers. Initially, Jahnavi felt bad about it and stopped talking to me. Then I told her if we don't have anything between us then why does she listen to such comments. *"Look Jahnavi, even God of cricket Sachin is hated by people across the world; then normal people like us will be hated by many."* She then understood and ignored them and everything became normal thereafter.

We became best friends and one day I asked her to come to my house. She first rejected my invitation and after some time, she agreed to come. So I went to IIT that day, she took permission from the warden and we came out. We went straight to our house and she was a little nervous since she was meeting my parents for the first time. My mother welcomed her and seeing her nervousness, my mom cracked some jokes and later we together ate lunch. After some time, I took her into my room, showed her around, and showed her all the medals and trophies I got in cricket. She was surprised by seeing the signed bat from Rohit Sharma and I explained to her that I had got that as a gift of my first double century in U-19 match against Baroda. So in the evening, my mother gave some sweets for her and we both went back to IIT. While she was leaving, I told her that the next day was my birthday and requested her to attend the party at Gulmohar and she agreed to join.

❖❖❖❖❖

That night, I was busy in getting advance birthday wishes from my friends. It was 11'o clock and I felt little drowsiness and logged out of my laptop and went to sleep. Thinking of party and gifts, I was halfway to sleep and my phone started ringing.

Triiiiiiing… Triiiiiiing… Triiiiiiing…

"Who could that be at this time of night?" I wondered. It was 12'o clock and I thought it might be one of my friend who called to wish me. When I picked up the call, I heard a voice that had fear of death in it.

"Help… Help… Somebody help me… Help… Help… Somebody help me…"

The voice sounded like someone who knows that he is in serious trouble. *"Where are you?"* I immediately asked. *"Are you ok?"* just then, the call ended.

Beep… Beep… Beep…

I didn't understand who it was but understood that one of my friends was in serious trouble and was being chased by someone. Then after a couple of minutes my phone again ranged.

Triiiiiiing… Triiiiiiing… Triiiiiiing…

It was again from the same number this time I was a little frightened to pick up the call. When I picked up the call, I again heard the same voice from the other side.

"Help… Help… Somebody help me… Help… Help… Somebody help me…"

"Who are you?" I immediately asked. *"Where are you, tell me something?"* just then, the call ended.

Beep… Beep… Beep…

Later I received the call a couple of times but I ignored and blocked the number. After sometime, I heard a similar sound from the hall. This time I started shivering and gathered all my strength and slowly opened the door. I could see a man stabbing in the dark and that man was crying for help. I called my dad and mom but none of them was picking the call, I didn't understand what was going on and switched on the light.

I could see blood stains all around and I could see my father was badly stabbed. But where has the person in the shadow disappeared I was looking sideways and when I turned back I saw he was dragging my mother outside of the bedroom. I could see she had also been stabbed and I got angry and took the bat and ran towards him suddenly the lights were off.

After a few seconds, the power was back and I was surrounded by the person and he just kept the dagger across my neck. He just said pray for the God it was your last day on earth. Before I count ten pray to God for your life. He started counting one, two, and three before he reached ten, I fainted.

After some time I opened my eyes, I could see my father and mother injured and blood strains all around. I asked them if they were alive and what was going on. Then Kishore came and explained to me it was just a prank that they played with me. Later my parents wished me and Kishore gave me a letter from Mumbai cricket association (MCA) inviting me to join the Syed Mushtaq Ali Trophy squad against Vidharba that Wednesday and an autographed bat from my idol Sachin. I was happy seeing these and later we had a celebration with cake cutting and some drinks and my sister also joined the party from Skype. I thanked Kishore for such an amazing party and after sometime, he left my house and asked me to meet him on Monday.

I woke up in the morning at 7'o clock and as usual mom made me delicious sweet and I ate and took blessings from my parents. I opened Facebook and I got a lot of wishes from my friends and relatives. But what bothered me a lot was that Jahnavi said she had some important work and will not attend the party. My sister again wished me and said she sent some surprise to me.

I asked mom whether the courier from sister came or not she replied that couriers will come at 9'o clock. So I kept talking to my friends and suddenly my phone started ringing.

Triiiiiiing… Triiiiiiing… Triiiiiiing…

I looked at it, it was an unknown number and looked fancy and I remembered the last night prank and rejected initially. Then I got a text message saying

"Hello Datta I'm Heidi your childhood friend call me once."

I was felt both shocked and surprised because Heidi was my childhood friend and I hadn't met her for years. I doubted again because it might be someone teasing again. But I got little hope and just thought to call her back because if it was really Heidi then I would be happy.

I called her and within a couple of rings she answered the call. She was really Heidi, she wished me and then asked me to come and meet her at the 7th table on the first floor of hotel Taj at 12:30 for lunch. I asked her how to identify her she said she will be wearing pink churidar and I said I will be wearing a blue shirt for the same.

I was still in surprise because nowadays people often make new relationships and forget the old ones and also mostly nowadays relationships are made by expecting something in return. Critics often say *"Poor person has no friends"* because most of the world became corrupt. Most people are loving things and utilizing people for their personal benefits.

Heidi was a very special one for me because she used to come to holidays for her grandparent's home and we used to play. We became very good friends and I used to spend most of the time at her house. During my class 6 holidays, I was playing cricket and she was watching my game. One of my friends hit the ball, I was running to stop the ball without bothering what was coming on the road. Suddenly a car came and I didn't listen to my friends and I was about to get hit by the car but Heidi came in middle and saved me. While saving me, she broke her leg.

After that incident, she never came back and as time passed her grandparents shifted. I told mom that Heidi called me, she felt very happy and asked her to bring home. After two hours, I got courier from my sister. It was just a small packing I was surprised to see because she usually sends me large gifts. So I opened and found a letter and a dairy and a greeting wishing me a happy birthday. So I just flipped through the book it looked like a diary and have topics like character, confidence, trust and more life-related topics. I didn't understand it and kept it aside and started reading the letter.

Dear Datta,

Today was your 18th birthday, and I wanted to commemorate that auspicious occasion with a letter to you, my little bro. Firstly I congratulate you on entering into your teenage.

As the only child and only grandchild in our family for three years, I was used to having all the attention and being the Queen of the Universe. Then you came and stole my spotlight, you Glory-Stealer! As they brought you into the house for the first time, I found myself bawling hysterically and screaming: "GOD, NO! WHY?! WHY ME?! SEND HIM BACK! GOD, HELP ME! FOR THE LOVE, WILL SOMEBODY TELL ME WHHHYYYYY?!" Every cunning 3-year-old knows that if you want something done, you have to do it yourself.

After time passed, I used to dress you up as a girl, take you to my school, and often make fun of you. Always we both used to quarrel with each other for small things like toys, remotes and at the end, you used to get punished by the dad. As we grew up, we used to share secrets and often made jokes on people. We screamed at each other and fought like cats and dogs. We fought fiercely with each other and fiercely for each other.

You always protected me from dad for doing silly mistakes and he used to punish you. I always thanked God for giving such a wonderful gift. So you might be confused about why I sent you a book. Actually, in teenage, we used to get many problems and we don't know answers to most of them. So to guide you I will not be available to you always so whenever you got any doubt to refer to this book. So enjoy the day and play well on your first T-20 Match in Syed Mushtaq Ali Trophy.

Yours
Big sister.

After reading this letter, tears rolled off my eyes and I couldn't control my emotions and called her and thanked her for such love and care towards me.

❖❖❖❖❖

A GREAT BLOW

It was 11'o clock but I didn't get ready for the lunch at hotel Taj. I took bath quickly and I went to my room and wore my jeans and started searching for blue shirt but I didn't find it. Then I asked my mom and she told me that it was in the washing machine. I was shocked and I didn't understand what to do. I took out the wet shirt and started ironing it; it took me 5 more minutes. It was already 12'o clock there and in hurry, I went to hotel Taj.

I was 30 minutes late, when I reached the hotel and I rushed to the first floor. I was searching for the 7th table from the entrance, a waiter came and asked me *"What do you want sir? How can I help you?"*

"Sir, I want to know where the 7th table is" I said. He showed me the way and I went there. I saw a girl wearing pink churidar with curly hair sitting there. I greeted her but to my surprise it was Jahnavi there, both of us were shocked.

"What are you doing here Datta?" She asked.

"I came here to meet my friend," I replied and look around but no girl was there. I started thinking that Heidi has left and I started blaming myself for being late. I was about to leave the first floor, I got a call from Heidi. I was in a question whether to lift the call or not because she might scold me. I answered the call with nervousness. She said that she was still waiting for me. I again went and started searching

the first floor but I didn't find any girl except Jahnavi. Seeing this Jahnavi called me.

"Are you waiting to meet anyone here?" She asked.

Yes Jahnavi, I was waiting to meet my old friend Heidi. She laughed and hugged me with tears. But I didn't understand what was going on. Are you Heidi I again asked in doubt?

"Yes you dumb brain I am Heidi aka Jahnavi."

I felt very happy, I gave the gift that I took and she wished me and gave a sketch of our childhood. We started discussing about our childhood and then she told she was moved to army school and in middle a waiter interrupted and asked for order. We both looked at each others' faces because the restaurant was new to us and we didn't know what to order. I asked him to bring menu and then we ordered some starters and then Biryani.

Then after some time I showed the letter of joining Mumbai Syed Musthaq Ali trophy's team. She felt very happy by seeing it and she congratulated and said she would be coming to watch the match. Then she told that she was an informer of a CID officer. I was shocked after listening this and also told that she was now working on drugs mafia. After 2 hours we left the hotel, I dropped her at IIT, and I went back to home. I told everything what happened there and my mother was shocked and felt happy for her.

It was Monday morning, I reached IIT by 7'o clock, and I went straight to meet Kishore in the college ground. He took me outside and we both took a taxi and we went to Mumbai Cricket Association. In the middle, he told me about the trophy and its history. We reached MCA by 8:30 and he took me straight to the selection committee.

I was a little nervous by seeing the committee and they initially took some physical tests and then later they asked me to wear pads and bat in the ground. I could see the players were practicing there and I stood in the middle of the ground. I faced an over and I sent a couple of balls over the rope and struck thrice to ropes. Then they gave a ball and asked me to bowl. I bowled an over with an average of 140kmph and couple of balls struck the wickets. On observing my batting style and raw pace they confirmed my selection for the squad. Then I was asked to sign a contract and I read it thoroughly and signed the contract.

In the evening, MCA made the official announcement of selecting me into their Syed Mushtaq Ali's squad in replacement of Manoj. Next day, the news was published in all the state and national papers. I received many calls from my friends for wishing me the best of luck. My sister and Heidi both wished me and as promised Heidi said she will be sitting in south stand in the first tier.

It was a big day for me, finally the day has come and I was confirmed to be in part of the playing XI. Being captain of team, Kishore showed me the dressing room and gave me a jersey with number 40 on it and named Datta at back. Rest of the players came to me and congratulated me for my first match and I placed all my equipment there and eagerly waited to step on the field.

Our team lost the toss and we were asked to field, and I walked into the field. My idol Sachin came and presented me the debut cap and wished me all the best, I took blessings from him and went into the field. I was looking for Heidi in the south stand, but I couldn't find her. It was 2nd over, Kishore was bowling and the ball was hit towards me, he called a catch. But I was a little nervous and I missed the catch and he came towards me and said

"Don't be too nervous Datta, even I was in the same position 3 years ago, pay your attention here!"

I started insulting myself and commentators also started commenting it was simple to catch and he missed it. 8 overs completed and opposition already scored 100 runs without losing a wicket. Then Kishore tossed the ball to me and asked me to bowl. I was a little nervous and I missed the Yorker and bowled a full toss. The batsman comfortably cleared the ropes. Then Kishore came and said don't become nervous, Datta relax and bowl according to your plan. Again I looked towards the First tier of South stand. There I pointed out a girl holding a poster with *"Came here to watch your play, Datta"*. I understood it was Heidi and I got some confidence.

The second ball I Bowled a Yorker, the ball hit the pad I appealed "Howzat" but empire didn't raise his finger. Kishore and keeper came towards me and asked me whether to take a review or not. I confidently asked to take the review and Kishore took the review. It was given out by the third umpire and all my team praised me for the breakthrough. Next ball I bowled a bouncer and batsman gave a catch to the keeper. 2 in 2 for me and I was bowling the fourth ball and more importantly hat-trick ball, Kishore made changes to the field and he went to slip.

I didn't know what to bowl on the hat-trick ball and I bowled an off cutter and the batsman had an outer edge and Kishore dived towards his left side and took a blinder. Everyone in the stadium applauded me and all my teammates praised me. I completed my 4 overs with 2 maidens and a 5 wicket haul. Our team managed to restrict the opponents at 160 in 20 overs. All the coaching staff and teammates congratulated me for my performance.

Our team's openers were good at the start and they managed to score 60 runs in the power play. In the next four overs, we lost 3 wickets in quick session and we managed to add 10 more runs after completing 10 overs. Slowly the required run rate came increasing and it was 30 needed off 10 after 5th wicket was down. I was asked to go and I took the bat that Kishore gifted me and walked into the field. I asked Kishore to give me the strike and he took single. It was my first ball and the ball clocked 140ks and I managed clear the rope over the long on. The last ball of the over I took single to keep my strike in the last over.

It was 22 needed off last over, a left-hand pacer was given the ball. The first ball I managed to clear the boundary. 16 needed off 5 now, the second ball he bowled a bouncer it hit my head and I was collapsed on the ground. A sudden silence in the ground and psycho came running to the ground it started bleeding and he asked me to leave the ground, but I rejected and said I wanted to bat. He gave some pain killers and did first aid and left the field.

It was 16 needed from 4 balls, I cleared the ropes in next 3 deliveries and Mumbai won the match and qualified for the playoffs with 2 league matches left. I was given the man of the match for my all-round performance and asked me to talk. While I was talking I was collapsed in front of presenter.

❖❖❖❖❖

Hours passed, I didn't know where I was and what happened to me, the last thing I could remember is talking with the presenter. I opened my eyes slowly, everything around me appeared foggy. I found myself on a bed surrounded by machines and I could see a nurse sitting next to me. I tried to recollect what happened the last night but I couldn't, the pain started increasing. I couldn't bear the pain and I yelled loudly with the pain. The doctor came running towards me and he checked my eyes and he gave me a pain killer.

After some time I came back into conscious and my parents and my sister came running towards me. I still couldn't understand what happened to me and I asked them and they told me everything that happened a few hours ago. Doctors checked me again and after confirming I am out of danger they moved to normal ward from ICU. Luckily I was out of danger but the doctor said I need to take at least 2 weeks rest. I couldn't digest it because I want to play more matches and win the trophy for Mumbai but this time things were not going on my side.

Soon, it became 9'o clock my sister gave me medicines and I ate some fruits and we were talking about her new job. In the middle, a girl came and interrupted our conversation. By seeing her my sister said *"What were you doing here and how did you know I am here."*

"Madam I came here to see my friend she replied."

I didn't understand what was going on and I looked at the girl, she was Heidi. How my sister knows Heidi, I was bit confused and interrupted them and said *"Sister, she is my classmate Heidi! It looks like you already have an introduction about her."*

"Yes Datta she is my informer in the city and she is helping me in a drugs case she tossed back."

Then I told about the long journey we both have to my sister and I introduced her. Heidi then came to me and gave a flower bouquet and wished me for my performance last night and wished me a speedy recovery. They both went outside and talked about some confidential things regarding the case and came back. Then my sister told me she has to go to the office and asked Heidi to look after me until my parents come.

We both didn't utter a word silence inside the room and I was thinking of Kishore bro. Then Heidi broke the silence

"How are you feeling now Datta?"

"Much better than before Heidi and now your presence made me happy."

"Yesterday I came here and saw your lightening sparks from you."

"I know Heidi, I saw you holding a poster in the south stand and seeing you I got much confidence."

"It was my responsibility to support you Datta because you are my best friend and I can say I support you even the entire world opposes you."

Listening that I felt very happy and thanked almighty for giving me such a great friend. We continued our talk and after some time, my idol Sachin came to meet me. I couldn't believe my eyes I pinched myself a couple of times thinking I was dreaming. But it was true he came and said

"How are you, my dear young boy?"

I was still in shock than with little nervousness and great respect

"I am doing well sir, soon I will back into action."

"That's my boy I liked your performance yesterday and felt sad after your injury, anyway happy seeing your recovery."

Then I thanked him and he asked me to take care of my health and advised me to participate in the next edition of IPL. While going he gave me a small gift and Heidi got a chance and took an autograph and a photograph with him. After some time my parents came and doctors gave some medicines and they discharged me.

In the evening I have opened the gift from my idol. There is a wooden box in it and a message saying *"Solve me to get opened"* on top of the box. It was a mathematical puzzle and I started working on it but I couldn't solve the puzzle. I started searching about the puzzle across the internet but I didn't find any clue. I worked more than 1 hour on it but still, I was unable to solve it and I kept it aside.

Again I started thinking about Kishore still no call or message from him. Then I called him but the mobile was switched off. I got a little tensed but I kept thinking positive about him. Then I opened my Facebook I got thousands of messages wishing me to recover well and I then understood that I became the talk of the country with yesterday's match. Most of them were from unknown accounts and some of them had sent friend requests too. I started talking with Heidi as usual and she informed me about mid-semester examinations in the next week.

Next morning I was watching news, suddenly a piece of breaking news came about the suicide of Manoj. He was banned recently from the MCA for 10 years for using steroids in the match. Then I got a call from an unknown number, it was from Kishore he asked me to come to IIT immediately. I didn't understand what happened to him because I was little tensed with his behaviour after the match and I can understand he was in a little hurry.

I immediately went to IIT and went to ground, I saw Kishore sitting lonely there. *"What happened Kishore is everything all right? Looks like you are in some tension."*

"Yes Datta, I committed a crime because of me a person died."

I didn't understand what crime he has done and who died. *"Tell me Kishore what crime you have done and who died because of you."* He started telling, *"Datta I think you know Manoj a player who was banned from MCA recently. Actually a week ago while we were playing against Chennai, a tough match for us, it was one of my worst performance ever. I played a test knock and I got out and without showing my face, I went straight to the dressing room.*

The dressing room was empty, I could hear my heartbeat, I started crying for my performance. After some time I calmed myself and changed my dress and kept all the equipment back in my kit. I was about to leave the room when I found a bottle that looked suspicious in the dustbin. I took it and started examining it, I smelled the bottle it had a strange odor. I again smelled the bottle, it had a smell of vinegar and I didn't understand who bought that and I started examining all the shelves of other players.

I found a syringe that had a smell of vinegar in Manoj's shelf and there was another small packet hidden. I opened the packet, there was a white powder in it and it had a strong odor of vinegar. It was drugs. I was shocked what does Manoj have to do with these and I started suspecting him. Then I got a beep sound from his bag, I took his mobile and started examining it. To my shock, he had contacts with drug dealers and he was also one of the dealers.

Then I started thinking about what to do, should I expose his crime or should I remain silent and indirectly support him. Then I asked my inner soul again and again and the only answer I got was to expose his crime. I took the mobile, syringe and then packet to the head coach after the match. He was shocked by seeing all these and the board decided to test Manoj. After some time the board tested Manoj and found he was taking steroids and they immediately banned him. The MCA board appreciated me and gave a badge of honor to me.

If I didn't expose him that day, now he would not commit suicide today."

Kishore started crying, I didn't see a boy crying and I tried to control him but he didn't. After some time he became cool, *"look Kishore you don't think like that because what you have done is correct. Don't ever think what you have done is a crime because you have made the world to know what exact truth is"* I said. After some conversation, everything became normal and then we got a call from MCA for some tests.

Before going to MCA, I immediately took Kishore to the hospital because his body was too hot. The doctors examined him and they told it was a normal fever and then they asked him to take medicines immediately. Then I went to the city medical store and took some medicines and Kishore took them. He became drowsy and started losing his consciousness; we both thought the effect would be temporary because of medicines.

It was afternoon when we reached MCA. All the players already came and waiting for their turn. Seeing me, my head coach took me to the director's room and there they appreciated my performance of the last match and gave a badge of honor to me. I was happy by seeing this and all the players congratulated and soon my turn came and all the tests were over and the board asked for Kishore to wait.

After 30 minutes, he came out with high disappointment and he started going out without paying attention to me. I didn't understand what happened to him and I asked the coach, he said that Kishore had taken drugs and he was banned from the MCA for the next 10 years. I was shocked after listening to this and I started following Kishore and I called him multiple times but he didn't listen and he went to IIT.

I followed him back and he went straight to the hostel and went inside. I again called a couple of times but he didn't listen to me. I went to the backside of the hostel and climbed the wall and started running to his room. When I reached there, he was standing on a chair and was about to hang himself. Seeing it, I was stunned and started shouting to stop him but he didn't stop and I broke the door. He was almost dead, he was out of conscious and I sprinkled some water and he came back into conscious and started crying.

"Kishore relax, I know you are not guilty and I can say that you didn't take drugs intentionally and someone might have injected them in your body," I said. *"No Datta, I don't have any hope in living without cricket and I can't raise my head in the society, please let me die,"* Kishore begged. *"I know Kishore, cricket is your life but just listen to me once, let's fight back and prove that you are not guilty. If you commit suicide now then this society will think that you have taken drugs."*

I went to Heidi and told everything that had happened, even she couldn't believe and she agreed to help us. Three of us started analysing how drugs entered the body.

"Look Datta, according to my knowledge drugs are mixed up with either food or in drinks mostly," Heidi said. Then I asked Kishore whether he had eaten food from outside college or did he have some drinks. He said he didn't drink or eat outside except at my home.

While we were clueless about how drugs entered his body, I got a doubt whether drugs can be mixed in medicines and asked Heidi. *"Yes, Datta, I forgot to say in recent years some companies are selling drugs in the form of medicines,"* she said. I got the picture of Kishore becoming drowsy after taking medicines from the city medical store into my mind. That's it, I explained the scene to both of them and we decided to test the medicines. So, I asked Kishore whether he knows any chemical engineer expert in the college.

"Datta, I know there is a friend of mine in the chemical engineering department and her name is Filomina," he replied. We decided to take her help and we told everything that had happened that morning and she agreed to help us. She took the medicine and started testing, it took 10 minutes of time and she confirmed there is an indication of drugs in the medicine. *"Datta let's file a criminal case on the store because we have proofs,"* Filomina said.

"No friends, if we file a case over them they change everything before the police ride on them. So let's find how these are manufactured, transported and who are their targets then we can certainly prove this as a crime and government will take required actions over them." Everyone agreed, but we all had little fear because big names may be involved behind this entire crime. *"Let's do a thing, let's identify where these medicines are available across the city and then we can proceed further,"* Heidi said.

So, we opened google maps and identified there were 10 stores in the city. Kishore and I changed our getups and we went to every corner of the city and purchased the same medicines and labelled them with the respective location. Then Filomina started testing the medicines one by one and after 3 hours of time, we identified there are 3 stores who were selling across the city. But these were located on various corners of the city and there was no connection between them. So again, we opened the google maps and started identifying the nearby places to these stores.

We found an interesting thing that these stores were targeting youth and sports people. We had decided to identify the source from which these were supplied to the store. One day we followed the empty supply van, it took us to a medicine manufacturing store where the medicines are manufactured. So we took the same medicines from the manufacturer and again Filomina tested these, but this time there were no drugs present.

Then we understood that someone was mixing up the original medicines and fake medicines and supplying them. Next day we again followed the same van but this time it was loaded with medicines. It changed the route and before entering the city, it went to a closed factory located outside the city and then later it supplied the medicines as usual. We came to know that there was something wrong happening in the factory, but how could we know what was going inside it, a question raised.

Kishore then brought a flying drone which was small as a housefly and very fast. It could record the surroundings with good quality and could be operated in a range of 100 meters. So we took the flying drone near to the closed factory and operated from 60 meters away. There were nearly 20 people, all armed with weapons and they were some people busy in making these fake medicines.

After recording for 30 minutes, we were spotted by a person and we ran from there. We reached the IIT safely and we got all the evidence to expose the crime.

Next day I called my sister and I explained the situation and she took me to the CID office. There, I told them everything that happened and we gave proofs to them and they appreciated us for our efforts. Next day, police officers raided the closed factory and caught all the criminals. Kishore got a call from the MCA and we both went and told everything that has happened and gave required proofs. After seeing all these, the board have reduced the ban from 10 years to 1 month on Kishore. Kishore thanked me for all the help and we four went for the restaurant that evening and celebrated our success.

PARTY IN THE HOUSE

It was the wedding anniversary of my parents the next day. Every year my sister and I used to give various surprises to them. But this year, she was not available due to her mission in Kolkata. So, I asked my friends to meet me urgently at the canteen to discuss this. Everyone came thinking I had a surprise for them.

"What Datta? Why did you called all of us, is there any special?"

"Nothing special but ..."

"Tell Datta what's urgent, do you have any problem?"

"Friends! I need all your help for organizing wedding anniversary party for my parents."

"Ok, I see it's not a problem. We all will help you." Kishore replied.

"Actually every year I and sister used to give them a small gift and we cut the cake. But this year, it's their 25th wedding anniversary so I decided to do it in a grand way by inviting some of our family friends and relatives. So, I need all of your help to organize the event successfully." I said.

"Ok Datta let's plan the event carefully and we will give full support." Heidi added.

"Ok, friends listen! I had a great master plan to work. First, let's select a good function hall for the event and then we should prepare a list of guests we need to invite. Later we can go for shopping for gifts."

We started searching the halls. Since it was marriage season, all the halls were full except a few which were very far from the city. We had a big obstacle before we could begin the planning.

"Datta why don't you use my back yard as function hall because we don't have many people!" Filomina said.

"Not a bad idea Filomina, but will your parents agree for this?"

"I don't know, let's go and request and see what's wrong." She replied.

We all went to Filomina's house. She introduced all of us to her mother. While we were talking, her father came and said *"I think you are Datta - son of Murthy,"* pointing towards me.

"Yes uncle, but how did you know me? I replied.

"Murthy and I were friends from childhood and at present, we both are working in the same company. What brings you here? he asked.

"Uncle actually I came here to take permission from you."

"Ask anything Datta! Don't hesitate!" He replied.

"Uncle tomorrow is my parents' 25th wedding anniversary, so we decided to organize a grand party but we don't have any function halls available. Thus I came to ask you to lend your backyard for the function." I replied.

"Ok Datta, not a bad idea. You have my permission but only on one condition."

"Tell me uncle, what's the only condition."

"You need to pay 1 rupee as rent and eat lunch here."

We all laughed and we agreed on the deal. He brought an album and started telling about my father and their silly acts during college and soon we all ate lunch and went back to the canteen. One thing was over; so next, we started preparing a list of guests we needed to invite. First, I called my sister and took all the relatives' phone numbers. We started calling one by one and it took over 2 hours of time.

Then I called Filomina's father and I took all the contacts of their friends and he told me that my father is a great fan of Sachin so why don't I invite him.

"Yes, Datta why don't you call him, because he had a good impression on you." Kishore said. But how could we, because we didn't have any contact details of him and how could we approach him. Then I kept the box that Sachin gave me in hospital on the table.

"What's this box Datta what is inside it?" Heidi Asked.

"Did you forget the gift that Sachin gave me another day?"

"Yes I remember, and I forgot to ask what's inside it."

Actually, it is a wooden box and there is a puzzle on it and I couldn't solve it. All of them took the puzzle and started their trails but none succeeded. Kishore started examining it carefully and after some time *"Eureka"* he shouted. *"What? Did you get the solution to solve it?"* I asked. *"Yes, Datta. These letters are Chinese which recently I have seen outside a tattoo shop."* We started searching for their meanings and we solved the puzzle.

It finally opened and there were chocolates inside and a small envelop. There was a quotation on it:

"Life is like a box of chocolates. Because problems melt you away but you should get stronger by overcoming all."

And there was another card on which a phone number was present and under it it was written *"call me."*

So, I immediately called the number and he picked up.

"Hello, may I know who this is?"

"Sir, I am Datta, Mumbai's U-19 cricketer."

"Oh, got you. How are you now? Did you recover?"

"Yes sir, much better than before and I need to take some rest. Sir, actually I want to meet you."

"Ok, Datta come to dinner today and bring your friends along."

"Thank you, sir." And I ended the call.

Finally, we got the address and it was the time to concentrate on shopping and decorating the backyard. Two of us went to shopping and rest of us decorated the backyard. Heidi and I took the list of required items and we went to Infiniti Mall.

❖❖❖❖❖

Infiniti mall is one of the biggest malls in our city. It is a huge building with three floors and each floor has its own specialty. On the ground floor, small stores and some food courts were there. On the first floor, it was completely related to men, and some kid stores. On the second floor, there were stores of famous brands related to women. On the last floor, there was a game centre and a theatre.

It was a 4'O clock in the evening when we entered the Infiniti mall through the main entrance. There were people coming and going continuously and because it was marriage season and companies were giving attractive discounts. Most of the people came here mainly to loiter. First, we decided to buy gifts for my parents. Since my mother liked handcrafted items, we went to the handicrafts store.

It was a small store and luckily, only a few people were there. There were numerous items of handmade wood, clay and metal items. I didn't have much idea about choosing gifts so I gave the baton to Heidi. She started viewing the items one by one and sorting out the good ones. Finally, she took a wooden box which was made up of teak and had a beautiful design of flowers. We both loved it and we then took some handmade flowers and left the store.

Then we went to a painting store and gave a photograph of my parents and asked them to make a portrait of it. We went to a book store in the meantime and I purchased some books of Indian authors and Heidi bought some biographies. We took the biography of Sachin to gift my dad and left for the first floor for men's wear.

We went to the Manyavar store which is famous for its wedding collection and especially for men's sherwanis and kurtas. I thought to take sherwani because regularly my father wears formals and kurta in functions. There were beautiful designs of sherwanis and I picked a royal blue kurta, while Heidi picked up pink ones with a different design. We debated over the blue and pink for some time and finally, we arrived at a decision to take the blue ones.

Then we went to Soch, a women's store located on the second floor. Soch was very famous for its quality and design of sarees. It was my mother's favorite choice for buying sarees and she often bought from them. As we didn't know much about the sarees, I video called my sister. She took thirty minutes for selecting the color and finally she took a pale pink saree.

Two hours passed and rats started running in the stomach. So, we decided to eat something and went to subway and ate some burgers and had some shakes in Starbucks and later went back to the painting store. He had completed the painting and we took a metallic gold coated frame for it. After a couple of minutes, we took the portrait and went back to Filomina's house.

In the meantime, Kishore and Filomina gathered all the decorative items and arranged a stage in the backyard. They also arranged chairs and covered the floor with carpet. We kept all the things inside the house and worked sometime in the backyard and left for IIT. I dropped Heidi and Kishore in the college and asked them to get ready by 8'o clock and went back to the house.

I had reached home. I took a shower, wore a red shirt, and told my parents about the dinner plan. Both of them felt happy and my mom gave a box of special ladoos to gift to Sachin sir. I took them, put them in the back seat, and went to fill up the fuel tank. There was a huge rush due to strike from the next day and I then went to the gas station and filled up with gas.

I was 5 min late to IIT than expected time and Kishore and Heidi were waiting there. Heidi wore a red churidar and looked so romantic than ever that I couldn't control my emotions.

"What Datta! Looking me in a different manner?" She asked.

"Nothing Heidi, your dress is too good and you are looking romantic." I replied.

Both of them kept laughing and I joined them and we went to pick Filomina. She too looked very attractive but that day, Heidi dominated her and I couldn't control myself without eying her. In the journey, I kept on eying her by adjusting the mirror and Kishore noticed that and he started cracking jokes on me.

We reached the house by 8:45 and I picked the box of ladoos and Heidi brought the sketch of her and Sachin drawn by her. We parked the vehicle and went to the gate and a guard stopped us and asked us to wait for some time. He went inside and after a couple of minutes, he came and allowed us after checking us.

There was a beautiful garden with various flowers and I could certainly feel the enchanting smell of the flowers. To its left, there was a small car shed and I could see some mango trees, neem trees in the lighting. There was a dog inside and it started barking after seeing us and the guard came inside and controlled it. The guard showed us the way to the guest room and asked us to be seated.

Then a servant came, offered us some water, and asked us to wait. After a couple of minutes, she took us inside the house. It was like a palace from the inside. I could see the photographs and some trophies kept for display. Sachin then entered. He was wearing red kurta and he looked so simple and calm.

He identified me and Kishore, and welcomed us heartfully. I then introduced both the girls to him and then I offered the box of ladoos to him. He opened the box and had one and distributed them among us. *"These ladoos taste too good Datta, who made these?"* He asked. *"Sir, it's my mom, she made these and these are famous around the city for their softness and taste."*

Then Heidi gave her the sketch she made for him and he took it. He opened it, examined it, and appreciated her for the sketch. He then took us to his trophy room located left of the guest room. There was a huge number of trophies and most of them were his awards from matches and explained his memories and experiences seeing them. I learned a lot from what he had told and decided to be simple and calm by remembering from where we came.

He took all of us to the dining room, there was a dining table for six and I could see the open kitchen to its left. He asked us to sit, I sat next to Heidi, and Sachin came and sat next to me. Then a servant came, arranged all the dishes on the table, and started serving. *"Don't be shy, eat as much you want because it is also your house,"* he said. He shared his life experiences and motivated me a lot and then we finished dinner.

"Sir, actually I came here to invite you for my parents' 25th wedding anniversary" and I gave him the invitation. He took the invitation, looked at it, and asked who was organizing the event. *"Sir, it's me and my friends organizing it in Filomina's backyard."* *"Ok, I see."* He then took his mobile, called his manager, asked him to cancel all his appointments in the evening, and said he will be coming. We were surprised to listen to that from him because he is a famous personality and he accepted our invitation. *"Look Datta, in general, I don't attend events regularly but your love towards your parents has impressed me,"* he said. I thanked him for accepting the invitation and took an autograph on the book that I bought that morning and left.

Next morning I went to Filomina's house and we all began finishing things for the event. Catering people came for checking out the place and we started arranging tables on the terrace of the house for dinner. They kept all their things and they left. We soon arranged lighting and a banner outside and on the stage. Then Filomina and Heidi started blowing balloons and Kishore and I attached them on the stage. Later we designed the stage with flowers and we spent over 3 hours and aunt called us for lunch.

"Ok, guys, I think we have done all the background work for today's event and thanks for your great support." I said.

"It's ok Datta, but there is another thing left and in the evening you will monitor the things, I will address the guests and Kishore and Heidi will receive the guests," Filomina said.

"Good idea Filomina. Let's stick to the plan," I said. We ate lunch there and I left for home.

I reached home and I wished my mom and dad and then gave them gifts. But I couldn't understand why father was not happy and he looked as if he was in a bit of tension. Then I heard a knock on the door and I expected that my sister came. I went and opened the door but there was no one and there was a letter in front of me. I took it and came inside but I didn't understand who sent it because there was no address on it. I was about to open it when suddenly my father came and grabbed it from me and went to his room.

I didn't understand and I took my remote and sent my robotic fly into his room. He was talking on his phone and was shouting and it looked like he was arguing with someone. Then he opened the letter and on it there was written

"Give the chip to me else you and your family will be killed."

Then I understood that someone was threatening my father but I thought to ask him about this the next day. Then Filomina's father Kumar uncle called my father and asked him to come for dinner. Everything was going as planned and I then presented them with clothes that I brought the previous day. I called Heidi and told everything that I saw and she told me to ask him tomorrow.

It was 7' O clock in the evening, my parents got ready, and we went to uncle's house. There at the entrance, Heidi and Kishore have welcomed us with flowers. Heidi looked very beautiful in her red saree and I tried to control myself again. They took us straight to the backyard and all stood and welcomed my parents. Filomina started addressing the guests and invited my parents on to the stage. Then Heidi and I danced on the stage and Filomina sang some melodies. Kishore entertained all of us with his magic skills.

Then the guest of the party Sachin along with his family arrived and my father felt very happy by seeing him and he sat in the front row. Soon one after the other came and shared their views and experiences with my dad and then the head of the company where my dad was working announced that they got promoted and transferred to Delhi. I felt both happy and sad by listening to that because I would have to stay in the hostel if my parents go to Delhi.

Now, Sachin sir took over the stage and shared some of his memories with his wife and their first days. Then Kishore again took over the stage and entertained all of us with his live magic for the second time. The time came and it was my father's turn to address the gathering. He spoke for almost 15 minutes and shared his best moments with my mom during 25 years and thanked all of us for attending the party.

We concluded the event in a good way and all the guests loved the party and enjoyed it. Sachin sir came to my parents and gifted a silver family tree, they thanked him for attending, and he took off.

The party concluded at 9:30 pm after dinner and my dad thanked all of us especially his friend Kumar for a wonderful party.

Next day I was going to college when again a letter came and my father went back to his room. I decided to find what he was hiding and went to his room.

"Father are you all right, why are you looking so tensed these days?"

"Nothing Datta, please leave me alone and go to college." He replied.

"No father, I am not going anywhere until you say the answer."

"Ok, make me a promise that you keep this confidential."

"Ok father, I promise you and I will not tell you, anyone, unless if I am in any trouble."

"Listen, Datta, what I am going to say is a top secret and I think you might not believe me. There was a person named Manoj and he is also a cricketer and recently he committed suicide. I think you know him and one day I was doing my job I got information about drugs trade and I went there secretly in a getup and recorded everything there and what is found is Manoj was nothing but Dr. J.

Dr. J has killed more than 100 people and was a most wanted criminal and 13 countries are looking for him. He always keeps on changing his appearance, now this time he took the face of Manoj but the only thing is he has a snake tattoo on his right hand. So, I started gathering all the pieces of evidence against him and I stored them in a chip and gave a copy of it to the police department. Instead, they gave it to him and he started threatening me to kill all of us if I don't give the original chip to him.

So, I don't know what to do and also I can't trust anyone now except my family and Kumar. So, Datta, I don't know how long I am going to live but I definitely want to see him before bars before I die. I will give you a small wooden box which tells you the place where I have hidden the chip. Don't try to break it, if you do so the box will automatically burn itself."

After listening to this, I was shocked and a little frightened and I understood that a great danger was going to come and I should be ready to face it myself.

A BITTER SWEET SMILE

The monsoons started and it was raining heavily outside and I was sitting in the canteen waiting for my friends.

"Hello Datta. I think you can play finals this Sunday." Kishore said.

"Yes Kishore, the wound was healed completely and I am expecting a call from MCA," I replied.

"Yes Datta, let's hope for the best and I am sure you will get it," Kishore said.

"What about you Filomina? Did your dad finish his packing?"

"Yes Datta, he packed all the things yesterday and I have to move to the hostel and he will come to join me tomorrow," she replied.

"Guys why don't we all stay at Datta's house so that we don't waste money and we will have all the freedom," Heidi suggested.

"Good idea Heidi, but who is going to do all the chores?" Kishore asked.

"Don't worry guys, Heidi and I will look after the kitchen and you guys just clean the house and bring the supplies," Filomina said.

"It is better that we keep a maid for all these things," I said.

Filomina took permission from Kumar uncle and I got the call from MCA and all my friends started praying for good news. I talked with them for 5 minutes and they confirmed my place in the Final and they asked me to join the next day for the grand final on Sunday. All my friends felt very happy after listening to that and we celebrated the moment with sweets and we were about to leave. Suddenly I got a call from my sister.

"Hello what's up, didn't hear from you from yesterday!"

"Datta something is wrong at home," she replied.

"What happened? Is everything fine there?"

"Father called me and he asked for help and I was busy in my mission and I was little frightened, so please go home quickly."

I started calling my father and my mom but none of them replied and a kind of fear started in me and my friends and I went to my home. The door was locked from inside and I pressed the bell but no one came and opened the door. We waited for a few minutes and Kishore and I started breaking the door. We finally managed to break the door and the moment I stepped in, all the things were thrown here and there. It looked like someone came and searched for something but the thing on my mind in that moment was that *where were my parents.* The fear rose in my heart and Heidi shouted loudly from the kitchen and we all ran into the kitchen.

There were blood stains all over the floor and there was a person in the blood badly stabbed. I went close to it, she was my mother. I was shocked by seeing that, started crying, and couldn't control myself. She was badly stabbed all over the body and I understood she was tortured and killed for something. I hand't seen a dead body before but I didn't expect to see my mother's body in this situation.

I heard a person calling my name from the bedroom in a low voice and I went inside where my father was lying in the blood stains and was stabbed in the same way and he called me near to him.

"He has done this. Don't leave him Datta," he said.

He took a promise from me to send Dr. J behind bars and he left his last breath. I started crying, I didn't know what to do, and I saw a graffiti on the wall with green painting saying

"I will kill entire family until you give me the chip."

Heidi called my sister and told everything that she saw and she told her to take care of me and she will be coming by evening. Then I called Kumar uncle and he cried over the phone. I didn't expect to see this in my life and I couldn't imagine my life without my parents. At that time, my friends stood as great support for me and I called the police.

The police came and collected the bodies and interrogated my friends and me and as usual, they said they will catch the criminals behind this. Kumar uncle came and tried to make me calm and said he will take care of me because both my parents are orphans. Then all friends of my father called me and showed their sympathy towards me. Sachin sir called me and asked me how it happened and said he will bear all my expenses from now on.

My sister came in the evening and I told everything that happened the previous day and I showed the box to her and she told me she can't help me because she was transferred to Goa. So, I decided to find the chip with the help of my friends and they had agreed to me for that. By the end of the day, all the rituals were completed and I had buried the bodies.

Soon we all started cleaning the house and we managed to put everything back to its place and Heidi cooked dinner for me. It was raining outside and all my friends left. I sat on the sofa and started recovering my memories with my parents while I was eating. Later I watched movies sometime and it became midnight as I was alone I felt frightened and went to sleep.

It was lightening heavily and dogs were barking on the streets. All the roads were empty and I was trying to sleep. Then I heard a knock on the door. I thought it might be my dream and I didn't attend it. After some time again I heard the knock and I slowly went and looked through the peephole. I found a man in raincoats and I opened the door.

"Who are you and what are you doing here at this time?"

"Are you Datta?" He asked.

"Yes, I am Datta what do you want?"

I saw a dagger in his hands and I was frightened and I was about to close the door and he pushed me. He jumped over me and was about to stab me and I shouted *"No! No! Please save me"*. I woke up, it was a bad dream I felt a huge relief. I went to the fridge and took a water bottle and opened the cap when again I heard a sharp knock on the door. I dropped the bottle on the floor and ran into my room and took a stump and slowly went to the door.

I went to the main door and looked through the peephole I found the same person I saw in my dream. I felt very frightened and I didn't open the door. *"I know you are inside. Open the door or else I will break it."* I heard these voices from the outside. I kept calm for some time and he stopped knocking the door. I was frightened and I called Kishore and asked him to come immediately.

Then the person from the outside broke the door and jumped over me. I managed to escape from his grip and ran into my room. He followed me, caught me, and kept a dagger on my neck.

"Who are you and why are you trying to kill me?"

"Tell me where the chip is? Where did you hide it?" He asked.

"I don't know about which chip you are talking."

"Don't act like I don't know that you are having the chip. Give it to me or else I will kill you," he threatened me.

I started pleading to him but he didn't listen to me and then he lost his cool and was about to stab me. I started praying to God and suddenly Kishore came and banged him on his back with the stump. He pushed Kishore back and ran away. We both chased him but he left in a white BMW car. I thanked Kishore for saving my life and requested him not to tell anyone about this.

❖❖❖❖❖

In the morning, I woke up very late than usual and I had only two hours to report at the MCA. I started searching for my cricket kit but it was not in my room. I came to the hall and it was lying on the table, completely packed. I was wondering who might have packed this so perfectly with all the equipment.

"Again you are late, this is bad on your part Datta. Go and get ready, you have to report by 9'O clock," said Heidi with her sweet voice.

I went to the bath and got ready and in the meantime, she cooked breakfast and kept it on the table.

"What Heidi! So early today, what's special?"

"Nothing Datta, I have shifted from the hostel and Filomina and Kishore said they will be coming this afternoon" she replied.

"Ok good, Kishore and I will use my room and you and Filomina can use that bedroom." She agreed to it and I ate breakfast, took all the things, and went out. Outside the main door, I found a letter and I went inside, kept it under my bed, and went to MCA. I reported in time, all the teammates were busy in practicing, and the chief coach called me.

"Good Morning sir, did you call me?"

"Come Dattu, sit. How is your health now?"

"Much better sir, I have completely recovered."

"Sorry to say that I have heard both your parents were murdered. Be strong at this moment and practice well," he said.

I thanked him for showing care towards me and I started my practice with ball. After some time, my batting coach came and kept a challenge of facing 20 overs without getting out. All the batsman wore pads and started playing. One by one batsman became out in less than 10 overs and I picked 2 wickets. It was my turn, I was last, bowlers almost lost their energy after continuous bowling, and the coach called for a small break.

During the break, all my teammates came and asked about my parents and showed their sympathy towards them. The break was over and I wore my pads and started playing. From the very first ball, I focused on the ball and I was not diverted at any moment. I successfully played 20 overs and the coach appreciated me and gave a medal of honor to me. We kept on practicing till the sunset and took rest.

In the night, I was talking with my friends and they said they would be coming to watch the match. It rained heavily overnight, the pitch became wet, and we were not allowed to practice during the morning session. The field's man started drying the pitch and mostly the pitch was damaged and all doubted for today's final. I started praying to God to make the match happen and luckily the sun shined and by the evening the pitch became dry.

In the night, over 25,000 people filled the stadium, all were waiting for the toss, and suddenly it started drizzling. The toss was postponed for about 2 hours and the rain stopped. The pitch became wet and umpires went and examined the pitch and confirmed the match. But the match was reduced to 10 overs on both sides. Our team lost the toss and we were asked to bat first.

The captain and coach kept on discussing about whom to send to bat. Due to 10 overs, they decided to send a batsman who can play the shots from the beginning. The coach asked me to open the batting and I was in surprise because in my second match, I was opening the batting. The non-striker walked into the ground and all were waiting to see who was going to open with the bat.

The movement I stepped on the field, all cheered me and even the commentators got shocked with the decision. A leg spinner opened the attack and I sent the first ball over long on. While I was facing the second ball, the wicketkeeper started abusing me and my family to divert my focus. Luckily I managed to defend the ball and again he did the same while I was facing the next ball.

I stopped the third ball, went straight to my non-striker, and told him about the same. He complained to the umpire about the wicket keeper and the umpire called him, warned him, and gave first warning. I continued my flow with a couple of sixes and boundaries and took a single off the last ball to keep strike of the next over.

The substitute came and gave me gloves, I changed the gloves, and I looked into the crowd to locate my friends. I found them on the south stand in the second tier and they were holding a banner saying *"It's going to rain sixes and fours because my friend opened the batting"*. I smiled after seeing it and I went to the crease to face the second over. A left-hand fast bowler came to bowl the second ball and I continued my form with a couple of sixes. Next ball, he bowled a bouncer, I played a pull shot but I took a quick edge, luckily, it fell in no man's land, and I took a double.

It was the 4th ball and I pushed it through covers and I scored 45 off 10 balls. The crowd was enjoying the show and commentators made the announcement of a record that if I managed to score a six of the next ball then it would be fastest fifty. Next ball he again bowled a length ball and I pulled it to the 2nd tier from where my friends were watching. Heidi caught the ball and kissed it and I lifted the bat and gave a flying kiss to them. I created a record of fastest fifty in cricket and all the players clapped for the achievement.

I got out on 80 during 5th over with a wrong decision taken by the umpire and I walked off the ground. All the players sitting there and my coaches appreciated me for the performance and after 10 overs my team managed to score 140 for the loss of one wicket. We got a good score on the board and we went to the field and I was placed in deep cover. The opposition team also promoted their middle-order batsman to opening.

Our opening bowlers did well and removed their openers in two overs and then I was asked to bowl the third over. The batsman hit two consecutive sixes of first two balls. The captain and wicket keeper came to me and advised me to bowl a slower one. Then I bowled a knuckleball and the batsman was bamboozled and lost his leg stump. In the next 3 balls, I picked a wicket and gave a double.

We have restricted the opponent at 70 runs for 8 overs and we won by 70 runs. I was given the man of the match for my 80 with the bat and 3-15 with the ball. Then I got the perfect catch award for my catch in the first match and our team lifted the trophy. I felt very happy because I made my team win the cup and all my teammates appreciated me for my performance.

I was very happy and lifted the trophy, pointing it to the sky to dedicate it to my parents. Our team players were busy posing with the trophy and I went to the dressing room and began packing things. Then came captain and coach and all the players who gathered for a cake cutting. The captain along with coach cut the cake and all the players ate and done a facial for the captain with the cake. The captain opened the bottle of champagne.

I was offered a glass but I rejected it and I got a call from Heidi. She asked me to come home early so that I could prepare for the next day's mid-semester exam. I went to the coach and told him about my examination, I wished him good night, and I came out of the dressing room. I came off the stadium and a mob fell over me for photographs and autographs. I couldn't deny them and I took over 30 minutes and satisfied their wishes.

Then a media channel came and asked me about the flying kiss after my half-century but I didn't pay much attention to them, took a taxi, and asked him to leave. In the middle of a highway, the car was stopped and the driver asked me to wait for some time so that he fixes the car. I went to a hotel for having something, there I saw a small boy cleaning the vessels.

"Hey you there! Come here once!" I called him.

"Yes sir, what do you want?" he asked.

"What's your name and why are you working here?"

"Sir, I am Raju and I am working for my mother," he replied.

"What happened to your mother?"

"Leave about me and my family. Tell me what do you want sir?"

He pretended to answer me and I promised him to help. He then took me to a poor hut a few yards away. The hut was very small with a few things inside. There was no fan even and his mother was suffering from a high fever. I took her immediately to the nearby hospital and I offered them some money.

"Ok, Raju where is your father and what is he doing?"

"Sir, my father was in jail. He was stuck in a robbery and police took him without proper pieces of evidence."

"Raju call me Datta and would you like to study?"

He said he wanted to study and become an engineer. I took him and his mother to my house. I told my friends everything, they appreciated me, and I took them to my outhouse. Raju thanked me for all this and I promised him to get release for his father from jail.

I sat in my room thinking about what to do in tomorrow's exam because I didn't prepare a single chapter. But I was in confidence because it was an English exam and I was sure I could fill up the booklet. Heidi came and started explaining what she had learned and helped me.

I woke up and I checked time, it was 8:30 and I was out of time. All my friends had already left and I left in a hurry. I reached IIT, checked my bag, and checked my things but there was no hall ticket and I went to the examination cell. There was a long queue but the principal saw me and called me aside. I told the situation, he issued me the hall ticket, and I left.

As I entered the hall, the answer sheets were being distributed. I occupied my seat in the first row and I was the last student to enter the hall. Soon the invigilator stood and began yelling instructions. Some students were whispering while he was giving instructions. He warned them strictly and he searched the pockets and asked us to leave mobiles and wallets outside the hall.

Soon, the bell rang, the question papers were distributed, and there was pin-drop silence. I looked at my paper and realized that I didn't know a single question and I decided to just fill up booklet. All the students started writing and I looked at Heidi, she was writing without turning sideways and there was no one in front of me. I started writing what I knew, I just kept side headings I knew and wrote stories from famous movies.

Half of the time was over; a student was caught copying from a slip of paper, which he had hidden in his socks. The invigilator concerned threatened to suspend him from examinations. The student fell on his feet and promised to discard this evil of copying henceforward. On the advice of the superintendent, the invigilator let off the student. After that, the students were scared to even turn their heads sideways and wrote the exam in silence.

As the paper was tough, most of the students could not attempt all the questions. Most of the hall became empty before the last 30 minutes and I didn't give a glance at questions and concentrated on filing papers. I was the last one to leave the hall and I filled the complete booklet. Soon, I reached out of the hall, my friends were waiting and they made comments saying I will be the topper of the branch.

I reached home, Heidi and I took Raju to nearby schools for admitting him but no school had accepted him. Then I called Sachin sir for his advice and he asked us to enrol him in reliance foundation. We went to reliance foundation and filled the form of admission and paid the fee. He joined in reliance foundation and his mother joined as a caretaker there for young children with the recommendation of Sachin sir.

Days passed, my exams got over and I prepared extremely well and wrote well. We were given a week's holidays and we were planning for a vacation. Then I showed them the box and told them all the things I knew about Dr. J. Initially my friends got frightened after listening to the story but later they agreed to help me. Then we all went to central jail along with Raju and our lawyer talked to him and he managed to set him free by winning the case. Raju and his mom thanked me for helping their family and his father said he will do anything for us.

THE MYSTERY OF THE BOX

It was a Sunday morning, I was dreaming of the chip, and then Heidi poured a bucket of water over me.

"Oops! Why did you pour water on me, Heidi?"

"You Kumbakarna! Sleeping the whole day, it is 12'O clock in the afternoon. Have you forgot we have to open the box?" she said.

"Sorry Heidi, I have a habit of sleeping more on Sundays."

"Go now, it's too late for your breakfast, I have to clean the room."

I went to the bathroom and started brushing my teeth when suddenly the bell rang.

"Heidi, go and look who is at the main door."

"Sorry Datta, I am busy in cleaning. Please go and check."

I went and opened the door. Raju along with his parents came.

"Hello Raju, what a sudden surprise!"

"Hello Datta, we actually came here to meet you."

I welcomed them and they sat on the sofa, I brought them some cookies and juice. We were talking normally and after some time again the bell rang. I thought it might be Kishore or Filomina and I opened the door. There was a letter and I was about to close the door when I found a feather of a bird. It looked very different and was in a combination of black and brown color with different patterns on it. I took them inside and kept them on the table.

"How did you get this feather, Datta?" Raju asked.

"I just found it outside the main door, do you know which bird's feather it is?"

"I know this feather since my childhood, it is the feather of the great Indian Bustard. While we were living in Solapur forest, we used to play with these birds." I was surprised by listening to this, I continued to talk with his father, and he went inside to see Heidi. In the middle of our talk, I found a tattoo of a snake on his hand.

"Uncle, that looks like a tattoo of a snake on your right hand."

"Yes Datta, it's our tradition coming from our ancestors," he replied.

"Oh! I see! Can you tell me more about it uncle?"

"Sorry Datta, please don't ask me more about it" he replied.

It was 1'O clock and the uncle stood up and said they will be leaving. Heidi came and asked them to have lunch and go but he said he had to go to his friend's house nearby. I called Raju but he didn't respond and I went inside to check. When I went inside the bedroom, I saw that he was looking for something.

"Raju come out, stop searching there, your dad is leaving."

"Ok Datta I am coming" he said.

He came out quickly and was going and I found that he was carrying something in his pocket.

"Wait! Raju, what's in your pocket? Show me now!"

"It's nothing Datta, Nothing!" He said.

"You shouldn't steal things, Raju. Show me what's inside!"

He took out a small box and I opened it. It has a golden key with a plus symbol on its handle.

"Where did you find this Raju?"

"I was searching around and I found this inside a cupboard." He replied.

He went outside and left with his parents after a couple of minutes. I was examining what this key might be and Heidi came inside. I showed it to her, she didn't understand about it, and we decided to go to a historian in the evening.

It was 5'O clock in the evening when we went to the city historian. The assistant stopped us at the door and asked us to wait sometime in the hall. I sat comfortably on the sofa but Heidi was looking at the paintings and ancient items displayed on the wall. Then she called me and showed me a photo. In the photo, there was a stone of rhombus shape and blue in color; ***"Stone of the King"*** the king of Akhel caves used to keep it, was written below it.

The historian came and the assistant called us inside. We went inside and sat in front of him. On the wall, there was a photo of the box which looked like the box my father gave to me. *"The Box of Key"* was written below it. I gave him the box and asked him to tell us how to open it. He examined it for about 15 minutes carefully and said

"Oh my god! It is that 'The Box of Key'! Where did you get it?" He asked.

"Sir, my father gave this to me a few days back and can you open it?"

"No, I can't and no one in the world is alive to open it," he replied.

He then took us outside and showed us the photo of the king's stone and said there will be a key to open the secret vault inside the caves of Akhel, but now those caves are closed.

"Sir, is there any other way to it?"

"I don't know much about them but there are tribes living in the forest of Solapur who know about it."

"How do they look, sir?"

"Till now no one has seen them but the thing is they have a tattoo of a snake on their right hand" he said.

Then I doubted that Raju's parents might be tribes from the forest. Later I gave him the golden key, he examined for some time, and this time he gave a straight answer

"It is the key of the box from the 16th century of Mughal Empire."

"Sir can you tell who has this box now?"

"Yes sure, two months ago a man named Murthy bought it at the city museum's auction."

We thanked him, more questions came in my mind, and I purchased the photo of the stone and came out. We decided to search for the box that my father recently bought at the auction in the house and went home.

We reached home quickly and the doors were already open, Kishore and Filomina had returned. We told them everything that happened and we started searching for the box. I kept the key for every lock of the house but none fitted.

"Datta I think its waste of time in searching for the box, I think Dr.J might have taken the box and forgot this key in hurry" Filomina said.

"No Filomina, I didn't find any ancient box in the house for 6 months."

"I think there is a secret place in the house Datta." Kishore said.

We got tired and we were going out of the room, suddenly Heidi shouted with pain.

"What happened Heidi?"

"I think I hurt my leg" she replied.

I looked down, she got injured and there was a small cut on her leg. I looked carefully, there was something like handle attached to the leg of the bed. I moved it down slightly, the shelf right to the bed moved slightly. Then I turned down the handle completely and the shelf moved completely.

"Look, Datta, I told you before about a secret place and here it is! There is a door behind the shelf." Kishore shouted.

"Yes Kishore, I didn't know about this earlier but the door is locked."

"Let's break the door so that we might find the box there." Kishore said.

We broke the door and there was a staircase which was leading to a basement and we took a torch and followed the way. We came down and looked around for a switch. I found the switch and turned on the light. There were blueprints pasted across the wall and some maps.

"Look Datta, picture of stone of the King on the wall!" Heidi pointed.

"Yes, Heidi but why my father was looking for it, I questioned myself and searched the room. At the corner of the room, I found the box."

"Friends here it is, the box of Mughal Empire."

"Check with that key Datta, we might find something helpful inside!" Filomina said.

I inserted the key, it fitted perfectly, and the box opened. There was a chip and some papers inside the box. We kept the papers aside, took the laptop, and inserted the chip. We opened the contents of chip and there were some images and videos and call recordings. We started examining the pictures; all were about his drug dealings and we found nothing from them.

We started playing video and there we saw the clear face of Dr.J and we examined the video carefully, there was a tattoo on his right hand exactly like the tattoo on the hand of Raju's father.

"Look guys, the tattoo is matching and I think Raju's father can identify him and he might be from the tribe" Heidi said.

"You are right Heidi, let's ask him tomorrow".

We clearly examined the video again and there was a sound in the background. Kishore then started tuning up and down the video sound and we heard the sound of the train clearly.

"I think Dr.J is living near a railway track." Kishore said.

"You are right Kishore but I didn't understand why did my father give the Box of the Key."

We examined the audio tapes and it was a conversation between Dr.J and another person. In that conversation, he was talking about a secret weapon that could turn any metal into gold and that anonymous person offered Dr.J a lump sum of 5 billion dollars. There were some other calls in which he was threatening my father for that weapon.

We took the papers we found and started examining them. There were some sketches of a weapon on them and in one of the paper, I found the sketch of the weapon with the king's stone placed on the top.

"We have found the chip Datta. Let's exploit the truth" Filomina said.

I took the computer and secretly copied the contents without call recordings into another chip and went to CID. We met the ACP and gave the chip and he was shocked by looking at those pieces of evidence and promised us he will arrest the Dr.J.

Next morning I was watching the television and then came breaking news and it was about Dr.J. The news was that Dr.J was killed that morning in the police raids and police seized the drugs worth a whopping amount of over 100 crores. I called my friends and they celebrated success.

"We have done this and we should take a long leave" Kishore said.

"No Kishore, we should not celebrate too early."

"What happened to you? Dr.J was killed and we have done our job and fulfilled your father's last wish!" Kishore replied.

"The job is not done yet Kishore and the real adventure begins now."

❖❖❖❖❖

I called Raju's mother and went to his school to meet them. We went to school and the teacher said to wait for him.

"Datta what adventure we are going to do?" Heidi asked.

"We are going to find the King's stone in the Akhel caves."

"Sound's good Datta, but we have to risk our lives." Heidi replied.

"Look friends, we have to find the King's Stone before anyone else so that we can safely keep it. If the stone is found by our enemies and if they get the blueprint, then they will convert everything into gold in the greed of money." Everyone agreed to help me in finding the stone and Raju came from his classes.

"Hello Datta, what brings you here?" Raju asked.

"I need to meet your father now, it's very urgent."

We took permission from the school and followed him. He took us to a closed underground drainage system. I didn't understand what his father was doing there.

"What are you doing here uncle?"

"I am saving my life from my enemies." He replied.

"Who are your enemies and why are they trying to kill you?"

"Please, Datta leave me like this and don't ask me about my past. Tell me why did you come here?" He asked.

I opened my phone, showed the picture of Dr.J, and asked him whether he knew him. He looked at the photo and was shocked.

"Why are you searching for him? Don't you wish to live longer?" He asked.

"Do you know him, uncle? Please tell me what do you know about him!"

"Memories that are good or bad stay with us till our last breath. Because of him, today I am living my life in this situation. It all happened 15 years ago....

15 Years ago

Every year we have a festival in the forest in which over 70 lakh people come and pray to the forest God. Some pray for the birth of children and some pray for good health. All believe that the God of the forest fulfils their wishes. People from outside the forest also join us and pray to the God.

On this auspicious occasion, my sister got lost in the woods and my brother and I went for her search. We searched the entire forest but we could not find her and we returned with empty hands. Seeing this, my father got tensed and started praying to the God. She returned after some time with some cuts on her body.

"What happened to you where have you been till now?"

"It's a long story brother. I was coming to the festival and in my way, I found a deer and I went away chasing it. It disappeared after some time and I found myself lost. So, I started tracing back my way, in the middle I felt very hungry and stopped at a tree. The tree had some fruits which were ripe and red in color. I climbed the tree and ate the fruits and I fell down the tree. I don't know what happened later, but I was saved by a boy. He saved my life and he brought me here."

I warned her not to go again into the forest alone and we were enjoying the festival. While everything was going good, a tiger attacked the mob. It killed over 10 people and people started running to save their lives. Then a boy came from the crowd, fought with the tiger, and defeated it. The people appreciated him for his adventure.

My sister called me, told me that he was the boy who saved her. She also told that she liked him and wanted to marry him. So I told my father and he agreed to marry her with the boy. I went to the boy to ask for his wish.

"Hello there! You braveheart!"

"Yes, tell me what do you want?"

I called my sister and they both talked for some time and the boy agreed to marry my sister. My parents married my sister with the boy in front of lakhs of people and all gave their blessings. They both were happy and they moved to Solapur.

We thought everything was going good, but one day when I went to meet my sister; she was tied to the pole with the ropes. She was beaten badly and treated as a slave in the house. She cried by seeing me and I took her to my father and told everything. Then my father called the boy and took him to the king of our tribe. The king ordered a divorce for sister and put him in jail.

He was sent to jail and my sister started living her normal life. After some days, the boy escaped from jail and came to my house. At that time I went to the town along with my brother. The boy killed my father and sister. I returned home and I saw blood stains on the floor and my father was lying dead on the floor.

I heard a voice from inside and my sister was lying in the blood and stabbed badly. She told me that the boy came here and asked my father about the secret of Akhel caves. But my father refused to tell the secret to the boy and he killed him. I cried by seeing them dead, escaped from there to save my life, and started living in the underground.

"Datta, the boy in the story is Dr.J and the secret he wants to know is about the hidden vault in the caves. So, he started chasing me from then and I kept changing my location once in a month."

"But uncle, how does your father knows about the cave?"

"Because he was a great grand grandson of the lord Akhel, the king of Akhel Caves" he said.

"Ok uncle, but now who can tell us the secret of the caves?"

"There are only two persons alive who know the secret" he replied.

"Who are they uncle and where can we find them?"

"One is Tanuj standing in front of you and the other is Anuj his twin brother" he said.

"Uncle, please tell us what do you know about the caves and the secret. Also, tell us how to go into the caves because we want to find the king's stone."

He agreed to tell us about the caves and took a promise from us not to tell others. He started telling *"Once up on a time…*

ONCE UP ON A TIME

Once upon a time, there lived a king named Raja who ruled the forests of Solapur and his kingdom was called *"The Kingdom of Las"*. It was named Las because the kingdom was full of forest, hills, caves, and waterfalls. People in the kingdom lived by producing and selling the products from the forests.

All the people there were very happy and the kingdom was the center for medicines and ores from hills. They exchanged these items with other kingdoms and earned money. The kingdom became richer and richer by selling its products from the forests. As wealth increased, the enemies increased rapidly and all the kingdoms tried to capture *The Kingdom of Las* but they failed due to its strong defense.

One day, one king from North India attacked the kingdom and captured all the forest. So, Raja sent his people and cattle into the caves and took his remaining army to the top of hills. From the top of the hill, his army attacked the enemy with arrows and the enemy was defeated. The North Indian king accepted his defeat and gave his daughter Rani to him.

Raja and Rani married and the North Indian king gave half of his wealth as a gift. Rani was very beautiful and a brave woman. One day the king caught a disease and became sick. Upon hearing this, kings from various kingdoms came together and camped at the borders.

She then turned like a dancer and went dancing in the king's hall. She started dancing and all the kings got diverted and the army of Las kingdom entered the camp. They killed the guards and wore their clothes and mixed poison in the food and all the army slept. Then they attacked the hall and killed all the kings. All the people in the kingdom appreciated for her bravery.

Everyone in the kingdom slept happily in the kingdom but the king couldn't sleep. He was getting old but he didn't have any children. He called doctors from across the world and used many medicines but there was no results. He started praying to God and he had built the temple for the God but still, he wasn't blessed with the children.

One fine night Raja got a dream and in that dream God appeared. He told that on the Himalayas there is a tree and if he can give fruit from the tree to his wife, he will be blessed with children. He made an announcement that if anyone can bring that fruit, he will give half of his kingdom. Many people came forward and went to the Himalayas but no one returned alive.

Years passed but no one brought the fruit from the tree and the fear of his trait increased more and more. He decided to go and bring the fruit himself but his wife didn't like him going. He left his kingdom in the hands of his wife and minister and started his journey along with ten soldiers.

He rode down the hills and forests for 2 days and reached Satpura range and decided to rest that night. The soldiers arranged the camp for him and he ate and went to sleep. One of the soldiers was guarding the camp and it became midnight and the guard became drowsy as time passed and he fell asleep. The fire at the camp exhausted but they were being watched by the enemies.

The enemies found opportunity and started coming towards the camp. Raja was awake at that time thinking about his trait and walking in his tent. He heard sounds and came out of his tent, but he could not find anything suspicious and he went back into his tent. He again heard the same sounds, listened to them clearly, and realized it was the sound of horses.

He started waking up his soldiers but they were sleeping and the enemies approached closer. He ran away to save his life into Satpura ranges. He found a cave and went inside it. It was dark inside and he took two stones and produced fire. He had no other way except going through the caves and he accepted his fate and continued to walk in the light.

While he was walking, he found a skeleton of human along with a chest near it. The chest was locked and he took a stone and broke the lock and opened it. He found gold coins, some jewels, and a rhombus-shaped blue color stone which looked different from the rest. He took that stone and decided to gift it to his wife if he returns home safely. He took some gold coins and some jewels along and continued his way.

He travelled further and further and finally found light from the other end. He ran towards it and there was a river flowing and he felt very thirsty and he drank water. He looked at reflection of his face in the water and he looked exactly like a slave in his kingdom. He followed the river and he finally reached out of the cave.

❖❖❖❖❖

He found a fisherman fishing in the river and went to him and asked to take him to the other side. He refused to take him but he was greedy towards the gold and demanded the Raja to give him 5 gold coins. Raja had no other option except to give him whatever he asks and agreed to give him the gold coins. The fisherman took him to the other end and the king paid him 5 gold coins. The king decided to buy a good horse and food and continue his journey to the Himalayas.

The king asked the fisherman about a market place to buy horses and the fisherman told him to cross the thick forest to reach a waterfall and down the waterfall, there was a city. He also warned him to be careful from the thieves. The king travelled for 2 days completely and reached a small hut. He decided to take some rest there and went inside. He dumped all his gold and jewels in a small pit under his bed to keep them safe.

He arranged a grass bed and slept the whole night there happily without any problem. Next morning when he woke up, he found himself tied to a tree and there were three persons standing in front of him. They demanded from him his gold but the king didn't open his mouth. They lashed him with a whip and were beating him badly and finally, he told them and they took all the gold except that blue stone.

The poor robbers didn't know the value of the stone and inserted it in the king's mouth so that he could not shout for help. The king became unconscious and the blood flowed from his wounds. He came closer and closer to death as time passed. Then a woman who was coming back with water saw him and saved him. She took him to her house and her father treated him.

The family offered him good food and the king recovered very quickly. He asked them the way to the market and the women took him to the market and she left. He didn't have any money with him to buy a horse except for the blue stone. He went to every jewellery shop and tried to sell the stone but none of them agreed to buy it. He had no other way to earn money except to work.

He went to each and every shop to find work but no one gave him any work due to his appearance and some said they don't give any work to strangers. He found only one shop at the corner of the market and he went there. There was an old man making swords and some other weapons. He took a sword, but the blade was blunt, and the grip of the sword was very poor.

"Hello sir, what weapon you want?" The old man asked.

"Sir, I came here in search of work, can you give me any work?"

"I can give you, but before that, do you know how to forge weapons?" he asked.

"No, but I will learn if you will teach me."

The old man agreed to teach him how to forge weapons. He started with basics and soon he taught advance methods and the king practiced more times on old metal before becoming an expert. The king went to other stores and observed their sales and he understood their sales were pretty good. He then studied the secret behind the sales and finally found that the designs were unique and attracted many people.

He started sketching the sword designs on a piece of paper first and then made a sword. The customers liked the designs and the sales increased. Soon the profit became ten times than earlier. The old man was very happy seeing those profits and he paid more and more to the king. The king finally got money to buy a horse but he realized that he wouldn't have a single penny after buying the horse and decided to work for some more time.

One day the king had decided to reveal the truth about him and his adventure to the Himalayas. But before that, he asked the old man about his family.

"Sir, I have been working here for months but I didn't see anyone coming and meeting you. Don't you have any family?"

"I used to have a wife and two children and my child used to help me here" the old man replied.

"But sir, where are they now? Did they leave you?"

"No, they didn't leave me but they left the world."

"How did that happen, sir?"

"A few years back, the king of this kingdom called all the men for a war against The Kingdom of Las. All the men joined the war including my two children. The war was won by The Kingdom of Las but my two sons died in the war. Listening to this news, my wife hanged herself in the house" the old man said.

After listening to this, the king couldn't say that he was the king of *The Kingdom of Las*. He felt guilty and the old man asked the king to tell about him. The king told that he was an orphan living in the woods. For the first time in his life, he couldn't proudly say that he was the king and told him that he was an orphan. The king decided to do something for the old man.

One day the prince of the kingdom where Raja was living came to the market to purchase a new sword. He went to every shop in the market and finally came to the old man's shop. Raja showed him the designs of the sword. The prince didn't like any sword but a design on the paper attracted his attention. The prince took the design and he liked the design and asked Raja to forge the sword of this design.

"I will forge the sword for you my lord but there is a problem."

"What's the problem in forging?" the prince asked.

"My lord, the stones shown in the design are real diamonds but I don't have any diamonds."

"That's a simple problem. Don't worry about it, my soldier will give you diamonds you need, but I need the sword at any cost" the prince said.

The soldier came and gave a pouch of diamonds that Raja asked for. Raja worked on the sword for three days and finally, he prepared the sword. Next day he went to the prince and gave the sword and the prince liked the sword and its design and gave him 1000 gold coins. Raja went to the shop and he gave the old man 900 gold coins for all his help.

Raja was finally happy that he had enough money to buy a good horse and continue his journey. He went to the shop and this time he purchased a healthy white horse and some maps and food required for his journey. After purchasing all these items, he was left with 80 gold coins. He went back to the old man for one last time and the old man wished him good luck in his journey and Raja continued his journey to the Kingdom of North India located in the north.

Raja had crossed the Vindhya mountain ranges and finally entered the kingdom of North India. He felt he had landed into heaven from hell because the kingdom of North India was ruled by his uncle. A guard watching at the watchtower informed about Raja's arrival to his uncle. His uncle welcomed him with a grand welcome and they went to the castle.

"What Raja, you are looking odd in appearance!" his uncle said.

"Yes, uncle actually I am in an adventure to the Himalayas."

"Why are going to the Himalayas? Are you searching for anything?" his uncle asked.

"Yes Uncle, I need to climb the mountains and get fruits from the tree and give it to Rani so that we will be blessed with children."

They continued their talk for some time and then his uncle took him around his kingdom. Raja loved the kingdom very much and most importantly everyone was looking happy in their appearance. But, he observed that they were in fear of something from inside and even his uncle looked the same.

His uncle arranged a grand dinner at his castle. The cooks had made all the famous dishes in his kingdom and Raja ate to his capacity after a long time. But Raja was not satisfied with the behaviour of his uncle at the dinner. He looked a little tensed and much in a hurry, so he decided to ask his uncle about it and went to his room.

"Uncle I want to talk to you."

"Yes, tell me what do you want to talk to me about?" his uncle asked.

"Uncle actually from today afternoon I am observing you and the people in this kingdom. They are looking happy on the outside but you all are very sad inside."

"Yes, there is a problem in this kingdom Raja. Thieves are looting our people and yesterday they have even looted our treasure" his uncle replied.

"Ok, that is a simple issue. Uncle do one thing. Tomorrow you make an announcement that you have found a blue diamond in the caves of Satpura Mountains. So, people will come to see it and the thief will also come to see it. In the night, he will definitely come to steal the diamond and we can catch him." His uncle appreciated his idea and next morning he made an announcement.

People from every corner of his kingdom came to see the diamond. They praised their king for his adventure and in the meantime, Raja observed each and every person but no one looked suspicious. Kings from various kingdoms came forward to buy it but his uncle didn't agree to sell it. Soon it became midnight, Raja and his uncle were secretly guarding the stone.

Then a man came from the entrance and he was covering his face in a cloth and wore a black outfit. Raja observing near the entrance, signalled his uncle to be alert. The thief went to the place where the diamond was kept for display. Both Raja and his uncle jumped over him at the same time. Raja held his legs tightly, while his uncle held his body. The thief tried to escape but Raja and his uncle held him tightly.

Then Raja shouted *Thief! Thief!* All the guards came to the spot with a lamp and tied him to the pole. Then Raja removed the cloth he was covering to see his face. They all became shocked by seeing the face behind the cloth. It was the minister of the kingdom, he agreed that he was the cause for all the robberies and the soldiers recovered the stolen items from him. His uncle ordered the soldiers to hang him for all his robberies and backstabbing him.

Next morning Raja again resumed his journey and before leaving his uncle called him and gave him a wooden box. He observed the box clearly, there were writings over it. These were written in ancient tribal language but the writings were not clear.

"Uncle, what is this wooden box for? These writings are not clear!"

"Raja, for your help yesterday in catching the thief, this is a small gift from my kingdom. And the markings disappear slowly when exposed to the atmosphere" his uncle replied.

"But, how can I make them appear again?"

"Since you are going towards Himalaya, you have to stop at river Ganga, wash the box with the water and the markings will be clear. Remember, only the water of Ganga with high purity shows you the reaction" his uncle said.

He thanked him and started his journey towards the river Ganga.

THE TRUTH OF KING'S STONE

Raja had reached the forests near the river Ganga, it was evening and he could see the beautiful sunset. The scenery of the sun setting down at the shore of the river was beautiful. The forest was so dense and dangerous with venomous snakes and wild animals. So, he had built a tent near the shore and decided to craft bow and arrows to hunt an animal for his dinner for that night.

He was walking through the forest, he found a rosewood tree, and he decided to chop the branches and make arrows from them. The tree was very tall and Raja started climbing the tree. He reached the top of the tree and he could see an entire view of the forest from the top. On his right, he could see the beauty of the river and on his left, he could see some smoke coming from the deep inside the forest.

He found some fine branches at the top and he took out his sword and chopped down the branches. He came down and took his small knife and started shaping the branches into arrows. He then finally sharpened the ends and got the perfect shape of an arrow. He again started walking to find some good trunk to craft a bow.

He walked and walked for miles but he couldn't find a small or medium trunk to chop down. But he was lucky and found some bushes of berries. Raja felt a relief and picked some berries and he comfortably sat on a stump near him. He liked the berries very much and was enjoying the juice from the berries. Suddenly he heard a cry from deep inside the forest.

He followed the voice and as he moved closer and closer the voice became louder and louder. He had reached the spot and there he found that a boy was tied up to a stick supported by two Y-shaped sticks on both ends. There were 3 people around the boy who were busy in putting a fire under the boy to boil him alive. Raja had nothing except few arrows and a sword and there were 3 people around the boy and they were armed.

He looked around and took some stones and threw them into the bushes right to him. One of the three observed the movement of bushes and came towards the bushes. The person observed around but found nothing and turned back to his way. Then Raja stabbed him a couple of times and the person fell down to death. There were 2 more persons left but the flame under the boy was growing at a rapid rate.

After some time, another person came to search his partner and again Raja attacked him back and chopped down his head. Now, there was only one person left and without waiting anymore, he attacked the last person and killed him. He quickly poured water on the fire and the fire stopped. He removed the ropes and poured some water on the boy to make his body cool. The body became cool and the boy came back to his conscious. Raja offered him some berries left with him and some water to drink.

"Who are you and what are you doing in this dangerous forest?"

"I am Akhel and I was wandering around the forest to find some food" the boy replied.

"Ok, Akhel! But where are your parents and tell me where you do live?"

"I don't have anyone and I am an orphan. I lost my way in the forest when I was 10 and an old man used to look after me. Recently these three man-eaters killed him badly. By the way, you are looking rich and what are you doing here?" Akhel questioned Raja.

"I am Raja, the king of Las kingdom and I am going to the Himalayas for an adventure"

"My lord if you don't mind can I come with you because I like adventures." Akhel requested Raja.

Raja accepted his request and they both went back to the tent.

❖❖❖❖❖

It was a full moon day and the moon was shining beautifully in the sky and Raja could hear some howling sounds of wolfs. Akhel caught some fish in the river and they were enjoying those fishes with some fruits and some coconut water. Then Raja took out the box and started washing in the river.

"What are you doing? Have you gone mad, the wood will become soft!" Akhel Shouted.

"Wait Akhel, wait some time and see the magic!"

Akhel didn't understand why Raja was doing like that and just nodded his head and continued enjoying the food. Raja cleaned the box carefully and started observing the box. There were markings on the box written in deep red color but he couldn't read them. Then Akhel took the box and observed carefully.

"I could read them Raja and it's a famous riddle in ancient tribal language" Akhel said.

"Oh is it? Can you solve the puzzle?"

"Yes sure, wait some time I will solve the puzzle."

Akhel rotated the blocks carefully and finally, the box opened. There were some diamonds inside the box and Raja thanked him. Raja then put back all the gold he had with him inside the box except that blue stone and Akhel closed the box.

"Why didn't you put the blue stone inside the box?" Akhel asked.

"I want to gift this stone to you and from now it is yours."

Akhel felt happy and he took the stone and kept the stone back into his pocket. They both talked for some time and soon they went back to sleep. However, Akhel couldn't get any sleep, he came out of the tent, and he went near to the shore, took out the blue stone, and looked through it.

He identified that the stone was not clear and had some kind of coating over it. He then washed the stone with the water of Ganga and looked through it. This time the stone was crystal clear and the view from the stone was very beautiful. He then took out the dagger that Raja gave him and looked it through the stone.

In no time the dagger was shining and he didn't understand why it was shining. He removed the stone from his hands and looked at the dagger. He was shocked by seeing the dagger because the dagger turned to a gold one. He couldn't believe his own eyes and he then took some metal pieces from the tent and looked at them through the stone. All the pieces turned into gold and Akhel couldn't understand what was going on.

He looked again around but none of them turned into gold. He then understood that the light from the stone can turn any metal into gold. He threw the gold into the river to remain unnoticed by Raja and keep this as a secret. He went back to his tent and slept the entire night.

Next day they began their journey and they initially crossed the river and reached the other side. They travelled for miles and miles and reached a very peaceful land where there were no wars. It was an independent land and people living there worshipped Buddha as their God. He never went to a land like that because the land he came from was full of wars and many people sacrifice their lives in order to capture the land of others.

He could see the Himalayas in the north and he continued his journey towards them. As he was reaching close to his destination, he was getting cold. At one point, they couldn't withstand the cold breeze and went to a nearby shop. Raja bought some woollen clothes to withstand the cold breeze and other equipment to climb the mountains of Himalayas.

They had finally reached the base of the mountain and both of them started climbing the mountain and managed to reach the top without any accidents. Raja found a lone tree with some fruits and he ran towards it and plucked a dozen of them. He finally felt happy in reaching his destination successfully and both of them walked back to his kingdom.

After years, Raja finally came back to his home and the people welcome him but he didn't find Rani. He called the minister and asked him about Rani. The minister told him that she was inside the palace and Raja told the minister to take care of Akhel and he went to the palace to see his wife after a long time. He reached the palace and went straight to his room to see his queen. When he stepped inside the room he was shocked and he could see his wife was sleeping and the doctors were doing the treatment.

"What happened to her?"

"My lord, she is suffering from an unknown disease and not only the queen, but nearly a hundred other people are also suffering from it" the doctor replied.

"Please, do something doctor. I cannot see her at this stage. I will give you anything you want but please cure her doctor."

"Sorry my lord, I cannot do anything and the situation is out of control" the doctor said.

Raja visited the people suffering from the disease and all the family members were crying and some of them even begged Raja. Akhel too went to see the people after Raja left and he found similar symptoms that of a mysterious disease that he suffered when he was lost in the forest. He then quickly ran to Raja to tell about the medicine for the disease.

"My lord can I tell you a solution?" Akhel asked Raja.

"Tell me Akhel, what is the solution to the problem."

"My lord, I suffered from similar symptoms when I lost in the forest and that old man gave me the juice from the fruits of the tree that we found on Himalayas" Akhel told to Raja.

Raja was in a dilemma now whether to save his wife and give the rest of the fruits to his wife to get children or to save all the people in the kingdom. He then remembered the words of his father that

"A king is the one who saves the lives of people, not the one who takes the life of his people."

So, he called the doctor and told him to extract juice from the fruits and give it to the people who are suffering from the disease. The doctor made juice from the fruits and offered it to all the people suffering from the disease. The medicine worked and slowly the people recovered and within a span of two days, they completely recovered.

Raja felt very happy seeing Rani back safely and asked Akhel to choose whatever he wants as a gift. Then Akhel asked Raja that he wants the love of his parents back. So, Raja then adopted him as his son and announced his decision to the people of the kingdom. All the people accepted Akhel as their young prince.

"Get up my son we have to go."

"Let me sleep some more time father, I was so tired after that long adventure." Akhel replied.

"No son, we are already late to the ashram of Guru Acharya located in the silent valley."

"But why dad? Why do we need to go there?" Akhel asked.

"First get up and pack your things, I will tell you in the way."

Akhel woke up and packed all his things and Raja took out a sword and gave it to Akhel. They started going into the caves, then again Akhel asked him why they were going to the ashram.

"Listen Akhel, being a king means saving your people at any time from enemies. To save our people from enemies we need some skills to kill the enemies.

Our kingdom is center for medicine and some forest products and to capture our kingdom, many wars happened and will happen in the future. So, being next king you should learn all the skills required to protect our kingdom from others." Akhel listened carefully but he was still in confusion what his father was saying. Then Raja told a small story that happened while he was a 10 years old boy.

Akhel when I was 10 years old, my father took me for hunting in the forest with him. Then I asked my father

"Father, why do we need wars and kill others? Why don't people live in peace?"

"So, my father didn't reply to me and he said to me to wait there for some time he will return back. I waited there for a long time and it became dark all around me but there was no sight of my father. I started searching for my father

but I didn't find him. I went deep inside the forest to search him and then a lion roared upon seeing me.

I started running and I found a huge banyan tree and I climbed it. The lion tried to climb up but it couldn't climb up and I started laughing seeing it. Then there was a snake on the tree hissing and I started climbing down slowly but there was a lion below. Then my father came and killed the lion and I came down safely."

"Look, Raja, you didn't harm the lion or snake but they want to eat you as their supper. So, if I didn't save you now you will be dead by either lion or snake. So, you need to learn some skills to protect yourself and protect your people from enemies. And wars are due to people's greed to conquer the world and some have greed towards resources. This greed is the reason for this blood shedding in the wars. If there is no greed for things, everywhere there will be peace."

After listening to this story, Akhel understood what his father told him and they both went to the ashram.

They reached the ashram and there were few students who were learning how to use a sword while some were practicing archery. Guru Acharya came and Raja took blessings from him and he introduced Akhel to him. Guru's followers came and took his luggage to a tree house and kept them in his room. Then guru took Akhel to training grounds.

There were hundreds of students nearly his age and most of them were wearing rich clothes and were looking very beautiful. Akhel went and joined them and some of the students looked at him as a servant due to his poor appearance. Every day they used to make fun of him and often they used to torture him mentally with their words.

But Akhel kept himself calm and never hurt them back and kept the focus on his practice. Every night he used to look at the things around him with the stone but nothing had changed into gold. But one day during one full moon night, the things around him turned to gold. He then understood that only the light from the full moon, when passed through the stone, can turn the metals into gold. Guru Acharya, who was offering some prayers during the full moon observed this wonder and he called Akhel.

"What you are doing Akhel? Why are you not sleeping in your tree house?" Guru asked.

"Nothing Guruji, I was watching the full moon."

"Don't tell lies Akhel. I know what you are carrying with you. Listen Akhel, you are carrying danger with you and whenever you use the stone to transform the things you will get a new problem." Guru said.

Then Guru gave him the water of river Ganga and asked him to clean the metals that he converted into gold. He cleaned the metals and the metals became normal. He advised him not to look through the stone and Akhel from that night stopped looking through the stone. Next day, a wolf entered the ashram and attacked Akhel and what Guru said became true. He got injured and he was asked to take some rest.

As time passed, one day Guru Acharya discussed about the archery competition in the kingdom of North India. He also told that famous kings from around the world come to participate and whoever wins the competition gets 1000 gold coins as a gift. No one in the ashram dared to give their names because they feared the competition from other kings.

Then Akhel asked the guru to take him to the competition. Guru was impressed for his determination because he was just 16 years old and he had never participated in the war yet. So he took him to the competition and everyone there laughed and criticized him and told him to go and play with toys. But Akhel just focused on giving his best in the competition.

The competitions had begun, more than 1000 kings around the world came to participate. Initially, Akhel felt nervous at aiming the target. Then Guru Acharya kept encouraging him and slowly he lost his fear, aimed at his target correctly, and had won the archery competition. Everyone across the world praised him and he donated all the 1000 coins to the Ashram. He had got the news that Raja was ill at home and went home.

THE HIDDEN VAULT

Akhel reached the palace to meet his father but he never expected it was the last time he visited his father. When he reached there, his father was lying on the bed. He was unconscious at that time and he observed him carefully and there were some kind of blue spots on his body. He doubted that someone might have given him poison. He called the minister to enquire about how that happened.

"What is happening in the palace minister? What are these blue spots on his body?"

"Prince, actually today morning I came to visit your father but he was sleeping and I knocked on the door but there was no response. So I called the guards and broke the door. He was unconscious so I called the doctor" the minister replied.

Akhel then called guards and he enquired them but they said they didn't see anyone near the room. He searched the room thoroughly and he found an iron hook. He examined carefully and understood it was a fishing hook and he kept it in his pocket. It became night and still, his father didn't come to conscious. The minister came and asked Akhel to go to sleep, so he went to sleep.

It became mid-night, everyone in the kingdom was sleeping when suddenly Akhel heard a scream of a lady. He again heard it and this time he confirmed it was his mother's voice and he ran into her room. The room was open and she was screaming and there was a person who was stabbing her. Seeing Akhel, the attacker jumped from the window and ran away. Akhel immediately ran to his mother and he pulled out the knife from her stomach.

His mother tried to say something but she left her life before saying it. Listening to the sounds, all the guards and minister came there. Seeing a knife in the hands of Akhel, everyone thought that he had killed her. The minister ordered the guards to catch Akhel but he had no other option except to run away and he also jumped from the window and escaped.

He ran into the caves and followed his way into silent valley to meet Guru Acharya, the only one who could believe Akhel at that moment. He went to the ashram and met Guru Acharya. Acharya told him to go and meet his granddaughter Lekha at the Foss waterfall and he gave a letter to Akhel to give it to her. Akhel took blessings from the guru and walked back to his kingdom to go to the waterfalls.

He had no other way to go to the waterfalls except to cross his kingdom. So, he had changed his getup and went to his kingdom as a culprit. Everyone in the kingdom was talking bad about him and then he heard that his father was dead and the minister was going to be the next king. And he also heard that the minister will be going to be crowned after 2 days.

He had less time in his hands and he quickly walked out of the kingdom without getting caught and reached the forests. He walked through the forests and he felt hungry and he looked around and found some mushrooms. He picked them and started eating them. After eating one mushroom, he fell off the ground. Poor Akhel didn't know that the mushrooms were very dangerous.

It was evening and Akhel came back into conscious and he could hear the sound of water falling from a height. He opened his eyes, he could see he was inside a cave and in front of him there was a river and a girl was taking warmth from a fire camp. He tried to wake up but he was suffering from body pains. So he took a fruit kept from the basket kept beside him and threw it outside. Seeing it, the girl came into the cave.

"You are lucky! I have never heard a person surviving after eating the mushrooms in the forest" the girl said.

"Thank you for saving me, I thought I would never see the world again."

"It's ok, I didn't see you here anytime. I think you came in searching for someone" the girl said.

"Yes I am new to this place and I came to meet Lekha, she is granddaughter of Guru Acharya. Do you know her?"

The girl laughed and said she was Lekha and Akhel gave her the letter that guru gave him. Lekha read the letter and said

"Ok, I understand you are in a problem and you need my help. Tell me what exactly happened."

Akhel told her what had happened and gave her the fishing hook that he found near the window in his father's room. The girl examined it and she said she would catch the fishermen tomorrow. She asked Akhel to take rest for that night so that his body pains will reduce and they could go the next day to meet him.

Next morning Akhel woke up and Lekha gave him some fruits and asked him to come out quickly. He came out and there were a group of fishermen who were busy in catching fishes. She observed everyone and confirmed that a fisherman was missing. She asked the nearby fishermen and one of them took to the missing fishermen's house. She told Akhel to wait outside and she went inside.

"Uncle Can you give me your fishing equipment to catch some fish?"

The fisherman gave her nets and a fishing rod and he searched his pockets for the hook. But the fisherman didn't find it and searched the entire house and said he lost his hook. Lekha confirmed that he was the person who lost his hook in the palace and called Akhel inside. Akhel took out the hook and said

"Is this hook yours? I found it."

"Yes it's mine, but where did you find it?" The fishermen asked.

"Tell me why did you attack my father yesterday night?"

"Are you joking, I was sleeping in my house" the fishermen replied.

"Then tell me how did this hook come into the palace?"

"I don't know how did it come, but I was sleeping" the fisherman said.

Then Akhel asked Lekha to search his house and she searched everywhere but there was nothing to suspect. She then lifted his bed and found the soil was very fresh and started digging it. There she found a bag and there were gold coins in it.

"Where did you steal them from?" Akhel asked pointing his sword towards the fishermen.

The fishermen agreed that he had come and attacked his father. He also agreed that he had killed his mother. Then Akhel asked why he had done that. The fishermen told that the minister gave him the bag of gold coins to kill his parents. Then Akhel understood that the minister wanted to become king. Akhel and Lekha took the fishermen and went to the palace to reveal the truth.

The palace was decorated with flowers and all the people were hailing minister as their new king. Akhel entered the palace and various kings of the nearby kingdom were invited and the Guru Acharya was about to crown the minister as the king when Akhel shouted loudly to stop. Everyone looked at him and Lekha bought the fishermen and Akhel asked him to tell the truth.

The fishermen agreed that he had killed Raja and Rani and told that minister gave him a bag of gold coins to do it. Then Lekha showed the bag and guru Acharya ordered the guards to arrest the minister and put him in jail. The minister was kept in jail and Akhel was crowned as a new king of the kingdom.

❖❖❖❖❖

Years passed, Akhel turned 22 and there were no wars, crimes, and deaths in the kingdom. The kingdom was in peace and people were happy everywhere. The ministers of the kingdom were suggesting that Akhel should marry a beautiful girl but he still wanted to serve his people. While everything was going fine, one thought changed the lives of people in the kingdom.

One day Akhel called the goldsmith and gave the blue stone and the diamonds that he found when he opened the wooden box to make a crown for him. He thought that this crown could be a memory for him about his adventure with his father. The goldsmith utilized all the diamonds and blue stone carefully and finally made a design of a crown with a blue stone in the center and remaining diamonds surrounding it.

Akhel liked the design very much and he appreciated the goldsmith with many gifts. He used to keep the new crown wherever he went. But he didn't think the crown will cause the bloodshed in the kingdom again. Enemies started moving close to the borders of the kingdom to steal the crown from the palace. No one expected that there would be a war for capturing the kingdom and keeping the crown on his head.

It all began with an attempt of stealing the crown from the palace. It was a full moon day and Akhel was standing near his window and watching the beauty of the moon. Then a guard guarding in the garden aimed at the king and released an arrow towards him. The arrow came like a thunderbolt and pierced into the hearts of a robber standing left to the king.

The robber fell on the king and the alerted all the guards and the robber was dead. Akhel was safe and he appreciated the guard for saving his life. Next day morning the forest was set to fire and the fire spread rapidly. The people started running for their lives and hundreds of people were dead and injured. The kingdom had lost 90% of its forest resources.

Then the kings from the north had attacked the kingdom. The battle for the crown went for over five days and Akhel managed to defend his kingdom but lost most of army and the people were still suffering from the fires. The inventories became empty and treasure became empty. Then he asked the help from the various kingdoms but none came forward to help.

He got help from the Ashram of Guru Acharya and all the people were sent to his ashram. Everyone was given food and shelter and some were treated with good medicine. Slowly the people started recovering but they were all in fear of death. Akhel didn't understand why suddenly after many years there was bloodshed in the kingdom. So he went to ask the Acharya to know the cause behind all that bloodshed.

"Guru I still wonder why all the bloodshed is happening all the sudden."

"It's all because of the danger you carry on your head" Guru replied.

"Danger on my head? I didn't understand what you are saying, Guru."

"I have warned you previously also about the blue stone. But, now you have kept it on your head like a crown. All these are because of the crown so don't ever keep it." The guru replied.

"But Guru is there any way to destroy it?"

"No! There is no way to destroy it but the only way is to keep it safe so that no one can ever take it."

Akhel had decided to keep it in a safe place so that no one could take it and carry danger with them. He kept thinking for the secret place the whole night and finally decide it to keep in the caves in his kingdom.

❖❖❖❖❖

"Good morning Guru Acharya. I came here to tell you an idea about safekeeping the crown."

"A very warm good morning Akhel, yeah tell me what idea have you got" Guru asked.

"Guru I am thinking to keep the crown inside the cave in a secret vault."

"Nice idea Akhel, but is keeping it inside the cave secure?" Guru asked.

"If we can block all the ways to cave then it will be safe."

Guru agreed to his idea but he kept a condition not to block the way from the Foss waterfalls. Guru also told that Lekha had a good knowledge of how to keep things secret and also making vaults from the ingots. Akhel agreed with him and he called Lekha to seek help from her.

"Hello Lekha I need a small help from you."

"Tell me Akhel how I can help you?"

"I need to keep the crown secretly inside the caves, so can you help me in designing the secret vault inside the cave?"

"Ok, I will help you out but we need some iron ingots." Lekha replied.

So, Akhel ordered his army to bring all the iron Ingots present with the blacksmith of the kingdom. They had bought the ingots but they were very few in number so he called the blacksmith and asked to melt all the swords and iron equipment in the kingdom and make the ingots.

The blacksmith collected all the metals and melted them in a furnace and made huge no. of ingots from them. They took all the ingots inside the cave and Lekha designed a blueprint of the secret vault and the workers started working and they worked for weeks and finally, they made a vault inside the cave.

Then Lekha gave a blueprint of the key that exactly fits the lock of the vault to a locksmith. The locksmith had designed the key and they were set to keep the crown safely inside the secret vault. Akhel had removed the crown and kept it inside the vault and he also kept some gold, some historical items belongs to the kingdom of Las. He looked at his crown one last time and Lekha threw all the blueprints inside the vault and closed it.

With the remaining ingots, the workers made huge walls and closed the entrances of the cave. Akhel then put the key into the wooden box that his father gave him when he met him near river Ganga. He gave the box to the Guru Acharya and he kept it near the Foss waterfalls. The forests began growing back and the people recovered and the kingdom became normal.

After some months, the Guru Acharya made a decision to marry Akhel with Lekha and both got married in mid-summer. Akhel was blessed with a girl and boy and he left the kingdom and he became a Guru at the ashram following the death of Acharya. The kingdom of Las became a center of peace as time passed.

THE RETURN OF EVIL

"Ok uncle, then tell us how can we reach the Akhel caves from the Foss waterfalls."

"No Datta I will not reveal it because I don't want to put you guys in danger" uncle replied.

"Please uncle tell us! I need to find that stone and protect it from enemies who want to use it to transform metal into gold."

"But I can't help you in this Datta! You choose the wrong person for help." Uncle replied.

"Please tell me, uncle, I want to protect it. And you have given me a promise to help me whenever I required your help."

Uncle walked around and looked at me once and he had no other choice except helping me.

"Ok, Datta I stand on my word so listen carefully. First you need to go to Foss waterfalls and then you need to follow the river until the shore. There you will reach a dangerous thick forest and if we can cross it we reach the caves." He replied.

I had understood the path correctly but I didn't want to put my friends' lives in danger. But, I knew that I couldn't do this alone without their help. So, I had no other choice except seeking help from them and I asked them for help. They knew that the adventure was not going to be easy and there was no guarantee that we could return alive. But they agreed to help me without thinking about their lives for a second when I asked them.

"Ok, where to start from?" Kishore asked.

"Kishore, first we need to open the box. So to open the box we need to get the water from the river Ganga. So first we need to go to Varanasi to bring water." Heidi replied.

"Good idea Heidi, I cannot come with you all the way to Ganga because I have a threat to my life. So, you guys come and meet me at Foss waterfalls with the water." Uncle replied.

"Ok uncle, let the adventure begin!!!"

❖❖❖❖❖

We had reached home to pack the things for the long adventure ahead of us. I was about to open the gate and a courier boy came to deliver a courier for us. I took the parcel and Heidi signed the paper and the boy left. I had opened the door and went inside and everyone went inside to pack their things.

I was a bit lazy to pack my things and I took the courier to see what was inside it. It was for Kishore and I called him but he was in the bathroom and asked me to open it. I opened the courier cover and there was a cover inside it. On the top, there was *"CONFIDENTIAL"* written in red bold letters. On the topmost left, there was a sender's address and it was from city super speciality hospital. I was shocked after seeing it.

"Who sent it Datta?" Kishore shouted from the bathroom.

"It is from city super speciality hospital Kishore."

I was about to open the confidential cover, Kishore came running out of the bathroom and grabbed it from my hands and went back into the bathroom. I didn't understand what happened to him and I went back to my room to start packing my things. I was about to open my cupboard and I heard a loud cry from the bathroom.

"What happened to you Kishore? Are there any worms inside your pants?" Filomina Laughed.

There was no response from inside, and he started crying louder and louder just like someone robbed a candy from the child. I called Kishore to know what happened but there was no response from inside. We all rushed to the door and began knocking the door to open the door but there was no response from him and he was still crying like a child.

"Let's break the door Datta we don't have time" Filomina said.

So, we took a few feet back and started running like bulls and suddenly Kishore opened the door. He looked emotionless and there was no confidential cover with him. We asked him what happened inside but he didn't even open his mouth and went inside his room like a programmed robot. We didn't understand what happened to him and we all searched inside the bathroom and nothing suspicious was there and there was no sign of the confidential cover.

I have never seen him before behaving like this. I went into the room, Kishore was sitting down at the corner of the room with a photo in his hands and was still crying. I tried to ask him what happened and what was there inside the cover but he didn't respond and asked me to leave him alone for some time. So, I left him and started packing my things one by one. I had decided to take the pot of my parent's ashes along with me so that I could mix them in the river Ganga.

It took me an hour to pack my things and I felt very hungry and went to the kitchen to get some cookies. Heidi was preparing lunch for us. I went inside and looked at the cupboards and found that cookies were over.

"I need something to eat Heidi, I am starving."

She didn't respond to me and was observing the tea shop from the window. I again asked her but there was no response. She continued to look through the window, I got angry and threw a tomato at her.

"What happened Datta, why did you throw it on me?" She asked.

"I was very hungry and I asked you many times for food but you were looking at that tea shop."

"Sorry Datta, Actually I was looking at that person who was wearing a red shirt there. He was observing our house this morning." She replied.

I looked at that person and I continued to observe him.

"Yes Heidi, he is looking at our house. But, I have seen him before."

"Where did you see him Datta? Do you know him?" She asked.

"I don't remember but I have seen him before for sure."

"Think Datta think, where did you see him?" She asked.

Yes! I got it. He is a senior inspector working in CID. I have seen him with ACP sir when I met him, I told to myself. But why was he observing our house? I decided to find out the reason behind this on my own.

"Sorry Heidi, I don't remember."

"It's ok Datta, wait for 5 more minutes, let us have dinner until then take these papads."

Next day I woke up at 6'O clock, it was my duty today to prepare food and clean the house. I was sleepless last night thinking about the officer who was spying upon the house. I was not good at cooking and still a beginner in making dishes. I decided to make bread omlet with orange juice which I learned from Filomina recently. I went straight to the kitchen and opened the refrigerator to take some eggs and bread loaves.

But my bad luck! There was only one egg left and just a few loaves of bread left. I had to experiment in the kitchen by making something by watching videos from YouTube. However, I didn't want to do any experiments now because we had to go to an adventure soon. So I had no other option than going to the nearby grocery shop and buying them.

I went to the shop and there was a long queue of people who were waiting to buy some milk. I had no other option than standing in the queue. I stood in the queue and it took 15 minutes to get my turn. I took bread, eggs and a couple of milk packets. I was returning back and I stopped a few yards near the tea shop. The officer was back on his duty, he was sipping tea and observing our house.

I had made my mind to exploit him but there were many people near the shop. I took my time until there was no one around the shop. After 15 minutes everyone near the shop left, even the tea maker had left to bring some milk. I went near him and asked

"What are you doing here officer?"

"Hello, Datta glad to meet you. I am enjoying tea here my boy. The tea is good here" he told.

"But officer I have heard that there is a city famous Irani chai shop in front of your house and you are drinking here by traveling 20km."

He was out of words and looking sideways to tell the answer then I added

"Don't put any pressure on your brain for answering me. I know you came here to observe me."

"Me? Observing you? Hahaha you are making jokes Datta" he replied.

"I know you are observing me, tell me the reason why are you observing me?"

"Stop joking Datta! I have many other cases to solve and I don't want to waste my time. But why would I observe you because you are not any suspect or criminal" he said.

"Oh really! Let me ask ACP sir about this."

I took my phone out and I was about to dial him when the officer said he will tell me why he was observing me.

"Datta this is confidential matter, let's go somewhere so that no one can listen to us." We both waited there until the tea maker arrived and I took him to my house.

❖❖❖❖❖

We entered the house and the officer asked me to close all the doors and windows so that no one could secretly listen to this. I asked him to be seated in the hall and I went inside to close the doors. Meanwhile, Heidi woke up and came walking into the hall. Seeing the officer, she shouted loudly my name. I came running to see what happened to her into the hall.

"What happened Heidi are you all right?"

"I am all right but what is this man doing in our house?"

"Relax Heidi, he has come here to tell something confidential."

Listening to our conversation Kishore and Filomina came walking slowly into the hall.

"What happened guys? Why are you shouting early morning?" Filomina asked in the sleepy state.

"Nothing to worry Filomina, come guys get seated." Heidi replied.

"I think you can start telling officer."

He looked at my friends being suspicious and he was still in doubt whether to tell or not.

"You don't need to suspect them sir, they are my friends and believe me they will keep this as a secret."

The officer stood up and removed his beard and mustache and he then removed his mask. Seeing the face behind the mask we were shocked.

"Tanuj uncle, you as an officer?"

"No you guys were mistaken. He is my twin brother and by the way I am Anuj" the officer replied.

"But, why are you hiding your identity for many years."

"I will have all the answers to your questions" he replied.

"Look guys, this is a very secret matter so keep this secret" he started saying. *"After the death of my father, my brother and I ran to Mumbai to save our lives. While we were searching for some employment, I got a job as an informer for the CID department. I gave correct information regarding criminals and got good fame in less time. Along with my fame, enemies increased and many of them threatened to kill me.*

So, then the ACP sir called me and suggested me to change my identity. So, then I changed my face and name and I was appointed as an inspector in CID. From then, I never met my brother again and I still don't know how he is now. But after many years recently when I was dealing with a robbery case I arrested him. I never imagined even in my dreams to arrest my family members. After his release, I have searched for him but I didn't find him.

Later I got busy with my work and then one day you gave us the evidence to prove Dr.J as a criminal. Then our department went to catch him but we were unfortunate that he was killed in that encounter. Media and all the people praised us for killing such a dangerous criminal. This is what you guys wanted to know but what I am going to say now will definitely keep you in shock for a long time. The real truth is that Dr. J was not killed in that encounter."

"What are you saying? Are you gone mad? You have given reports to prove he is dead and even the media has shown his body" Filomina asked Anuj in shock.

I was still in shock and Anuj continued

"Guys calm down, even I got shocked when my informer told me about this and didn't believe this until I saw him with my eyes. One day my informer called me and asked me to come to the port. I went to the port and there he took me into the sea to some distance and gave me binoculars to look at the boat that is away from us. I looked through them and I couldn't believe what I had seen.

I saw Dr.J and the boat was well guarded by his men armed with guns. I had informed this to ACP sir and he said this was to be kept secret and we both reopened the case of Dr.J and we both started working on the case secretly. We started tapping his mobile with his mobile IMEI number. We used to get information regarding drugs deals early and we use to catch the criminals.

But one day we heard about the king's stone and a person had offered him 100 crores for that stone. We were shocked listening to that much amount for that stone. After that call, he called a local goon to follow you and kill you after taking **"The Box of Key"** *from you. ACP sir then ordered me to keep an eye on you and protect you from enemies."*

"But how did he escape from you uncle?" Heidi asked.

"That's the question I'm asking since I have seen him. By the way, you don't need to call me uncle because I'm still a bachelor and treat me as your friend" Anuj replied.

"*Ok Anuj, will you help us in finding the king's stone?*"

"*Ok, sure I will help you and protect you till my last breath*" Anuj replied.

With the joining of Anuj, we got our full strength and we decided to start our adventure.

IN SEARCH OF PURITY

We had packed all the things and Anuj had also bought his luggage but still, we didn't plan which way to go. We had started searching for flights but all the flights were full. Some of them had vacancies in business class but the ticket cost was too high and none of my friends agreed to burn their pockets. Anuj being a senior inspector in CID contacted all his contacts but he managed to get a seat for himself.

We had no other option rather than choosing a train journey. We started searching for trains, the prices were low but the journey was very long. At an average, the journey was 26 hours while some trains were taking 30 hours of time to reach Varanasi.

"I think we need to wait until the flights are available" Kishore Said.

"It's a bad idea Kishore, we shouldn't wait for more time. We are already late because enemies are watching you and someday they will attack us and take the box from us" Anuj replied.

"In that case, it is better to choose a train with the shortest travel time" Kishore replied.

"In that case, there is a train at 7:50 am and it is exactly one day of travel and we will reach tomorrow at the same time" Heidi replied.

"Good idea Heidi, but I have heard that there is a delay of 2 hours and we will be reaching there by 10 in the morning. But the temple will be opened till noon only so we need to choose another train." I suggested.

"Ok, in that case, we have to travel in Mahanagari express this afternoon" Heidi replied.

I opened the IRCTC website and luckily, we found tickets in 2nd tier Ac compartment. I booked tickets and the train was at midnight at 00:10 and we would be reaching Varanasi at 4:40 after traveling 28 hours without delay.

We had reached the Chatrapathi Shivaji railway station by 11:30 PM. Many taxis, scooters, autos, and rickshaws were standing in rows inside the compound of the Railway Station. A few traffic policemen were standing there to assist the incoming and outgoing vehicles. There was a huge crowd of people coming and going. Some of them were returning from faraway places while some of them were local people who were going back their home.

We entered the railway booking counter to inquire about the platform on which the train arrives. At the booking counters, there were long queues of people who wanted to purchase railway tickets. Some policemen were on duty to maintain order. They also kept a vigil on anti-social elements like pick-pockets and confidence tricksters.

Kishore said he would stand in the queue and after 5 minutes he came back and told that the train would be arriving at platform no 1. We took the escalator and went to the platform no 1. There was a huge crowd of people standing near the general compartments. Some of them were sleeping on the platforms while some were sleeping on the benches. The waiting halls were full so we walked towards the 2nd tier AC compartments.

There were few people sitting on the benches and we found empty benches and we sat there. It was 12:00 in the midnight, and then an announcement was made informing that the train will be arriving 20 minutes late. I was feeling a little bit hungry and I went to a nearby stall to get some biscuits. Heidi also came along with me to drink some coffee. I took some biscuits and she took coffee for her and we went back.

Suddenly, there was an announcement that the Mahanagari express from Mumbai to Varanasi was arriving at Platform no. 1. All the passengers on the platform stood up. Coolies picked up the luggage on their heads. Parents held children by their arms. When the train arrived, some young passengers boarded it when it was still in motion. We boarded it when it stopped and we kept our luggage on the top.

I took the bag which had the box inside it and kept in my arms and sat near the window. After some time, the train began moving and one by one everyone started sleeping. But, I had decided to guard the bag that night and all my friends slept. Anuj was also awake along with me and I took a novel and started reading it. While he took a magazine and began reading it.

❖❖❖❖❖

It was a 1'O clock in the afternoon and I woke up. There was a book in my arms and I realized that I had slept the whole night without safekeeping the bag. I looked around and the train was stopped in a railway station. I observed carefully and it was Itarsi written on the signboard. None of my friends were there beside me. I slowly woke up and went to the bathroom to brush my teeth.

I had completed brushing my teeth and came back to my seat.

"You Kumbakaran slept the whole night without having any shame" Heidi scolded me.

"Sorry Heidi, I got sleepy while reading but where is the bag? Is it safe?"

"Yes, it is safe right there." She pointed towards the bag.

I quickly took the bag and opened it to check the box. I found the box and some chocolates along with it. I took some of them and ate them. After some time the train started moving slowly. Kishore and Anuj had returned, but Filomina didn't board back.

"Where is Filomina Kishore?" Heidi asked.

"She is buying some food items, Heidi." Kishore replied.

The speed of the train began slowly and we started shouting. She turned back, seeing the moving train she started running but the train almost crossed platform. She was too far from our compartment but continued running and luckily she entered the general compartment. After some time she was back to our compartment. That incident had deeply scared us and we didn't move an inch until Varanasi had arrived.

After a long journey of 1500 kilometers for 30 straight hours, we reached Varanasi at 6'O clock. Heidi and Filomina woke us and we took the entire luggage and departed out of the train. The station was very crowded; many people were still sleeping in the compartments. Anuj hired a taxi and then we left for the hotel. In the midway of our journey, we ate Jalebi, Kachori, and Sabzi for breakfast. These were famous breakfast items in Banaras.

We reached the city hotel, which was built very close to the bank of the river. We took two separate rooms to get ready to go to the temple. We went to our room, the room was very spacious and it was very neat and tidy. I opened the window and there was a perfect view of the river. I could see some people praying along its bank while some saints were doing prayers and some boats in the river.

I never forget that view of the river and the cold breeze of wind in my life. We got ready very soon but Kishore was not willing to come with us. He looked very tired, so Anuj asked Filomina to look after the box and Kishore. We kept all our electronics and I took ashes of my parents and came out of the hotel.

Varanasi is the new name of Banaras. Varanasi is located on the banks of the mighty river, Ganges and houses several shrines within its territory. Once, Mark Twain, a great author quoted that *"Banaras is older than history, older than tradition, older even than legend and looks twice as old as all of them put together"*.

Some of the most famous holy shrines of the city that people visit here are Kashi Vishwanath Mandir, Durga Temple, Tulsi Manas Temple, and Bharat Mata Temple. Among all these temples, Kashi Vishwanath Mandir is the most popular one and enshrines the Jyotirlinga of Shiva. History reveals that this temple had been destroyed twice by invaders but still it is standing tall with all its grace.

We went to "Vishwanath Gali", a street that takes us to the temple. There we had bought some pooja stuff and sweets to offer to Lord Shiva. Kashi Vishwanath Temple is one of the most famous temples in Varanasi. It is also known as the Golden temple dedicated to Lord Shiva. This temple is having great religious importance to the Hindus because this temple is one of the 12 Jyotirlingas of Lord Shiva and this one is 12th.

We have reached the main entrance of the temple and the security guards checked us thoroughly. There was a queue of people standing to see and offer prayers to Lord Shiva. We stood for 30 minutes in the queue and finally, we got our chance to see Lord Shiva. I was delighted to see him and the beauty of the temple. Heidi offered pooja for Lord Shiva and soon we came out.

There were various small temples such as the Kaalbhairav, Avimukteshwara, Vishnu, Vinayaka, and Virupaksh Gauri located in the temple premises. After the main temple and Jyotirlinga visit, we visited all these temples and wisdom well inside the temple premises. I purchased some clothes and items inside the temple and went to Ghats.

Another most charming aspects of Varanasi is the long line up of Ghats alongside the river. These Ghats looks awesome at dawn. Many people offer the pooja here and mostly many people come here to mix the ashes of their relatives to make their souls to rest in peace. People believe that the person goes to heaven when his ashes are mixed in the holy river of Ganga. This is the reason Varanasi is called as *'Gateway to Salvation'*.

We hired a boat to go to one of the Ghat and in the middle of the river I asked him to stop the boat and we took the water of Ganga in a bottle. Then I asked him about the ghats for performing the rituals. The boatman informed us that among all the Ghats of Varanasi, Dashashwamedha and Manikarnika ghats have special significance. Manikarnika Ghat symbolizes the creation and destruction (it is framed as the main cremation ghat of Varanasi) whereas Dashashwamedha Ghat is famous for its evening 'Ganga aarti'. So, we asked him to take to the Manikarnika Ghat and he took us.

The Ghat was very crowded and the boatman took to one of the priests. The priest asked me to wear traditional wear and I borrowed from one of the vendors and I wore traditional wear for the first time in my life. I then sat in front of him and he then asked me the names of my parents and other details. He offered some prayers for them and I finally mixed the ashes in the river and prayed to Lord Shiva for my parents to make them a way to heaven.

We waited there till the evening and the boatman took us to the Dashashwamedha Ghat for Ganga Aarti. The Ganga Aarti is very beautiful and we hired a photographer there and he took some amazing snaps of us. The photographer took his time and developed the photos and we paid him enough. We boarded back in the boat and he took us to the shore and we came back to the hotel.

❖❖❖❖❖

We reached our respective rooms and Kishore was still sleeping and we kept all the things there and Filomina came with the box and we all gathered and Kishore also woke up. I took the water of river Ganga and I sprinkled a few drops. There was no appearance of the marks.

"I think we need to pour more water, Datta" Filomina said.

Then I took a small cup of water and poured on the box. Even then there was no appearance of marks.

"Pour that entire bottle, Datta" Heidi said.

Then I poured the entire bottle of water and we waited for some time but there was no change of color again.

"Stop wasting water, Datta. Can you recall what Tanuj uncle told us?" Heidi asked.

"No Heidi, I don't remember what he told."

"He told us the water should be very pure and the marks disappear slowly when exposed to air" Heidi replied.

"You are right Heidi, but how can we purify this water now?"

"Don't worry guys I know how to purify them. I had learned during my 2nd year. But I need some things." Filomina replied.

"Tell me the list of things you need to purify the water."

"I need some tiny pebbles, fine sand, charcoal, and some filter papers" Filomina replied.

Anuj and I went to the shores of Ganga and I picked up some grain sized pebbles. Meanwhile, Anuj filtered the sand to make it fine. Then we went to Vishwanath Galli and we purchased some pieces of charcoal. He then took me to Banaras Hindu College to the chemistry lab and we took some filter papers and returned back to the hotel.

Filomina took all the things and he kept them aside. She took a water bottle and removed the bottom part and then opened the cap and placed the filter paper inside the bottle. She poured the powdered charcoal into the bottle then she poured the fine sand and finally pebbles on the top of the sand. Finally, she poured the water into the bottle to it purify.

We waited for half an hour and finally, the water came down of the filter paper. The water became crystal clear and I took the box and poured the water on the box. We waited for a few more minutes and the marks became clear and visible. Anuj took the box and he observed clearly.

"Can you read it Anuj?" I asked him.

"I can't read them Datta but I know these alphabets, these are ancient tribal alphabets" he replied.

"Can anyone read these?" I asked him.

"Yes, my brother Tanuj can read it. He learned it from my father." He replied.

We packed all the things back and started our journey to Foss waterfalls to meet Tanuj uncle.

THE BEAUTY OF THE KING'S STONE

Waterfalls are one of the most beautiful sights to see around the world. Though there aren't many waterfalls in India like other countries, some available waterfalls are worth giving a visit. But I was lucky because I was going to visit the waterfalls for the first time in my life.

It was 8'O clock in the morning and we reached the Foss waterfalls. There were some tents around the shores and some people were already enjoying the water. The birds were chirping and some people were fishing on the other side of the shore. The sound of water falling from the top was very beautiful. It was like a piece of music and the water was very pure and looked like milk.

Anuj took us towards the other side where people were fishing. There I could see Tanuj uncle from a distance and we all went to him.

"Hello, uncle how are you doing?"

"Hello, Datta glad to see you early. Have you found pure water of river Ganga?"

"Yes uncle we have found the pure water from river Ganga."

"Ok Datta, but where are the others? What happened to them?"

"Nothing to worry uncle, they are bringing a surprise for you."

"Surprise! I like surprises Datta."

We were talking and then my friends arrived along with Anuj. Seeing Anuj, Tanuj uncle felt very happy and they both hugged and he started crying in happiness. They both talked for some time and Tanuj uncle thanked all of us. He then took us into his tent and I gave the box and purified water of river Ganga.

Uncle took and he poured water carefully and the marks appeared clearly. He then slowly moved the slides on the top and the top of the box moved sideways. He took the key outside from the box. The key was shining and made with gold and there were some diamonds on the bow of the key.

"Look guys I am going to keep the key back because if Dr.J managed to catch us he could not open the box" uncle said.

"Ok uncle it is a good idea, I think we need to go to the Akhel caves."

"Yes Datta we have to first take a boat to go to the caves." He replied.

We felt very hungry and Tanuj uncle fried some fish and gave some fruit. The fruits were very tasty and I have never tasted them before and finally, we ate some nuts. He then took an axe and took all of us to the backside of the waterfall.

There was a huge number of bamboo trees and some banyan trees which were very old. Uncle started cutting down the bamboo trees and Anuj climbed the banyan tree. Anuj asked us to pick the twigs that he throws down. He threw a large number of twigs and we sorted them and finally picked 15 of them which were very strong.

Uncle finally managed to get a bamboo of 40 feet tall and then he started breaking it into equal parts of 6 feet each. We kept all the parts and began tying them with the twigs. Uncle went back and again chopped a bamboo of 40 feet and he again chopped it into equal parts. We worked for an hour and we finally made a bamboo boat. We placed it in the river and we all boarded it and the brothers started sailing the boat towards the caves.

We reached the dense forests and we were 10 kilometers from the caves. Tanuj uncle and Anuj became tired and we decided to rest there for the night. As time passed, the forest became darker and darker and it became completely dark all around after the sunset.

"Listen, guys, this forest is very dangerous and there is a tribe that lives here that eat animal flesh and human flesh as their meal. So don't go alone inside the forest" Anuj warned us.

Tanuj uncle had built a tent for us and we cooked some food and we all ate. So, we had arranged a campfire to get some warmth.

"Guys shall we have some fun?" Filomina asked.

"What can we do here in this dense forest Filomina?" Kishore asked.

"Shall we play truth or dare?" FIlomina replied.

"Sounds good Filomina, I am ready to play" Kishore replied.

We all agreed and I took a glass bottle and we sat in a circle formation and I kept the bottle in the center and spun the bottle.

Everyone was eagerly looking where it stops. It stopped at me and I was dead.

"Tell me, Datta, what do you choose? Truth or Dare?" asked Heidi.

I looked sideways on what to choose and finally said Truth.

"Ok tell me who is more beautiful I or Filomina?" asked Heidi.

It was one of the worst questions a girl could ask a boy. If I said Heidi was beautiful, Filomina would get hurt and if I said Filomina was beautiful, Heidi would get hurt. I was stuck and they both were looking to kick me if I said the other was beautiful. So, I took my mobile and opened a picture.

"Not you both, this girl is beautiful."

"Who is she, show to me!" Filomina asked.

"I showed the picture of a monkey which was wearing a dress and posing."

They both got angry and started throwing stones on me and I started running but they caught me.

"Tell me who is beautiful?" Filomina asked.

"The eyes that can see you can't speak and the mouth that speaks can't see." I replied.

Both were confused and left me. I escaped but I told them that both were beautiful finally. We again sat and I spun the bottle again and this time it stopped at Filomina.

"Tell me Filomina, Truth or Dare?" I asked.

"I choose dare," she replied.

"Ok, Filomina go deep inside the forest and come back after 10 minutes." Kishore said.

"No, Filomina. Don' accept this challenge. It is very dangerous, Kishore, tell another one."

"But Filomina already stood and started going, so I asked Heidi to go along with her."

I didn't know why Kishore had given her this challenge, I spun the bottle, and this time it was Kishore's turn. He chose truth and I was in a dilemma what to ask him. Then I got a question and I asked.

"Ok, Kishore tell me what is inside the cover?"

"Which cover Datta?" he asked.

"The cover that you got from the city super specialty hospital."

He was stunned and asked me to ask another question but I did not agree with it and I asked him to tell the truth. He then accepted to tell and took a promise from me not to tell others.

"Datta I have cancer and I will die tomorrow. I was suffering from bone cancer and the doctor has told me that I will be dying soon." He replied.

I was stunned after listening to this and slowly tears started rolling from my eyes without my notice. I got emotional and started crying and Kishore consoled me.

"Ok, Kishore we can't change our fate but tell me what is your last wish before you die."

"I don't have any wish but I want to tell the truth" he replied.

"What was that truth tell me Kishore?"

"Since the first day of my college I loved Filomina but she treated me as a friend. We became good friends but I never told her fearing that she would refuse

me and our friendship will be lost. But before I die I want to tell her that I love her." Kishore replied.

"Don't worry Kishore, I will help you in this matter."

❖❖❖❖❖

I was sleepless last night and the sun rose back and Tanuj uncle woke up all of us at 6'O clock and we packed all the things. He removed tents, fire camps and we started walking towards the caves. The birds were chirping and it was drizzling but we continued to walk. We walked for 2 kilometres and stopped at a huge tree.

The tree had a large number of fruits which were ripe and Anuj climbed up and gave us the fruits. They were very tasty and juicy and I took some more and kept in my bag and we continued walking. We were just 8 more kilometres away from the caves. I was praying to God to make this journey successful without any more dangers ahead. But we were unfortunate; we fell into big danger.

While we were walking slowly towards the cave, I got hurt by a stone and it started bleeding from my left leg. Anuj stopped seeing me and he started giving me first aid. My friends continued to walk slowly. After going at some distance, they were struck in the trap set by some hunters.

We went towards them after listening to a scream; they were stuck inside a large net hanging down a tree. Anuj asked me to wait there and he started climbing the tree, but he jumped down without helping them. I didn't understand why he had done that and he told me to hide behind the bark of the tree.

A group of people came to the tree and all were armed with guns and they were covering their faces with masks. They opened the net and asked all my friends to follow them and they took them away.

"Who are they Anuj? What are they doing here?"

"I thought this was a trap by the hunters but it was not by them. I don't know who are they but they look very dangerous." He replied.

"How can we save our friends from them?"

"Don't worry Datta! I gave a watch to my brother! Using it, we can trace where he is." He replied.

Anuj opened his laptop and he started tracing the location. The signals were weak and after several attempts, we finally found his location. I took a photograph of the location and we started following the location. After travelling some distance we finally reached a camp. Anuj took binoculars and climbed a tree and watched the camp.

"Are they safe Anuj?"

"Yes they are, but we can't rescue them because they are nearly 20 men armed with guns." He replied.

Then I got an idea and I took my flying robot and I asked Anuj for a poison. He took some leaves and made the juice and I applied it to the tail of the robot and flew it inside the camp. I attacked one by one with the robot's tail like a mosquito and one by one the men collapsed. I then moved the robot inside and there was only one person left in the dark and he was consuming weed and my friends were kept inside a cage.

I moved the robot quickly towards him but for our bad luck, the robot fly fell down. The charge of robot fly was over and we had no other option other than attacking him by ourselves. So we went inside the camp and Anuj said he would be attacking him from back and I went straight into the tent where my friends were there.

"Welcome, Datta! I knew you would come here someday and meet me. The man who was consuming weed spoke."

"Who are you? How did you know my name?"

"Don't you know me? How could you forget the person who killed your parents brutally?" The man replied.

"Dr.J, why did you kidnap my friends?"

"Don't you know Datta? Ok well, tell me where the key is?" Dr J. replied.

"Which key are you asking for? I don't know have any key with me."

"I expected the same answer from you. Ok then, what's the use with you and your friends. Let me kill your best friend Heidi."

He took the gun out and was about to shoot her. I had no other option rather than giving him the key. He started counting 1.. 2.. 3...

"Wait! I shouted loudly. I will give you what you asked, don't kill her."

"That's my boy. Come give it to me." Dr J. replied.

I took the box out and opened it and gave him the give. *"Please leave my friends now"* I begged him.

"No, I am going to kill all of you. I will kill them one by one in front of you." He replied.

"No Dr J., please leave them. Kill me if you want." I pleaded to him.

He didn't listen to me and he was about to shot Heidi, then Anuj shot him in his head from his back. Dr J. collapsed and he came near him, he shot him twice and I took the key and I released all my friends. Everyone was safe and we came out of the camp and we continued to walk.

After walking 5 more kilometres, we finally reached the caves. After seeing the caves, I felt very happy because I was going to fulfil my father's last wish. We went inside and it was dark inside and the bad smell of bats was coming. We took a torch and we walked inside the cave. After walking some distance we finally reached the vault.

I inserted the key and opened the huge vault and we finally found the crown of lord Akhel with the King's stone shining in the centre. We took the crown out and there were some diamonds and ancient coins and some ornaments. We had finally found the treasure and saved it from the hands of evil. I was happy for fulfilling my father's last wish.

EPILOGUE

Varun: What a great adventure to protect the treasure of Akhel caves by you and your friends! I appreciate you and your friends for your efforts. But, what happened to Kishore? Did he express his love for Filomina?

Datta: After finding the treasure, we all were happy and celebrating in joy but Kishore collapsed on the ground and the blood was coming from his mouth. Everyone was shocked seeing him in that situation. Except me, no one knew what happened to him. I started crying and my friends kept asking me what happened to him. I shouted, *"Kishore has cancer and he is going to die today."*

Everyone started crying and Kishore continued spitting blood. Then I slowly said that he had one last wish to fulfil. Everyone asked what his last wish was. He wanted to express his love that he was hiding from Filomina. She went towards him and Kishore slowly stood on his knees and he took some flowers from his pocket and said: *"I Love You Filomina".*

"I know Kishore that you love me from the 1st year but I expected someday you will tell me. But I never expected that you will express it on your last day." She accepted his love and they both kissed. After sometime Kishore left his last breath and he died. We all cried for some time and we had no choice rather than accepting his fate. We then buried his body inside the cave and we went back sadly.

Varun: I am sorry Datta, I didn't expect this thing. Have some water.

Datta: Thank you, sir.

Varun: Are you ok Datta? Shall we continue?

Datta: I am ok sir. Yes, you can proceed sir.

Varun: What happened next Datta?

Datta: After the death of Kishore, I felt I became like a statue and started living lonely…

Tik! Tik! Tik! Tik! Tik! Tik!

Varun: Sorry Datta our episode's time is over. Let's continue our show in the next episode. Readers, don't go away. Stay tuned for the next episode same day and at the same time.

To Be Continued…